A
Harlequin
Romance

OTHER
Harlequin Romances
by MARY BURCHELL

THE OMNIBUS
Has Arrived!

A GREAT NEW IDEA
From HARLEQUIN

OMNIBUS — The 3 in 1 HARLEQUIN only $1.50 per volume

Here is a great new exciting idea from Harlequin. THREE GREAT ROMANCES — complete and unabridged — BY THE SAME AUTHOR — in one deluxe paperback volume — for the unbelievably low price of only $1.50 per volume.

We have chosen some of the finest works of four world-famous authors . . .

VIOLET WINSPEAR

ISOBEL CHACE

JOYCE DINGWELL

SUSAN BARRIE

. . . and reprinted them in the 3 in 1 Omnibus. Almost 600 pages of pure entertainment for just $1.50 each. A TRULY "JUMBO" READ!

These four Harlequin Omnibus volumes are now available. The following pages list the exciting novels by each author.

Climb aboard the Harlequin Omnibus now! The coupon below is provided for your convenience in ordering.

SONG CYCLE

by

MARY BURCHELL

HARLEQUIN BOOKS   TORONTO
WINNIPEG

Original hard cover editon published in 1974
by Mills & Boon Limited.

© Mary Burchell 1974

SBN 373-01834-7

Harlequin edition published December, 1974

Printed in Canada

1834

CHAPTER ONE

"You don't think – " Anna regarded her mother with something between hope and doubt – "that this time Dad really might have brought it off?"

But her mother shook her head with humorous finality.

"Three times in our married life your father has been certain he has composed a masterpiece, Anna. Not to mention several other occasions when he was moderately sure. He wasn't right any one of those times. I can't believe success is just waiting round the corner for him now."

"Many of the great masters had their failures first," Anna claimed defensively.

"But few battled on into their late fifties without some sign of their latent genius," countered her mother with a smile.

"Poor darling!" Anna laughed reluctantly, but she gave a sigh of real sympathy too. "He *loves* it all so much."

"It's never enough just to love it all." Mrs. Fulroyd, who had cherished no more than a moderate liking for music throughout her rather difficult life, remained realistic. "You have to have vision and judgment – in the right proportions. And if you ever hope to hear your work performed, you simply must have some regard for what is practical in that respect too."

Anna nodded regretfully and both fell silent, each recalling in painful detail some of the more grandiose and improbable scenes in which Kenneth Fulroyd's unperformed operas abounded.

"He's going to be desperately disappointed if his work

is turned down once again," Anna said at last.

"But he always recovers with astonishing speed and resilience," her mother replied consolingly. "Don't worry, dear. Most of the time he's very happy, playing the organ and teaching his beloved music at the school, and indulging in his dreams between whiles. That's the secret of happiness, I sometimes think – to work hard at what you love and to dream your dreams. Anyway, that's what makes your father happy."

Anna wanted suddenly to ask if her mother were happy too. But, for no reason she could define, she was all at once afraid of the answer. For it occurred to her, for the first time in her life, that her mother was looking older and, somehow, less positive than she once had. Which was queer, when she came to think of it, because it was her mother whom she had always associated with all the confidence and security of her happy life.

True, it was her father's enthusiasm and knowledge which had inspired her with the longing to train as a singer. But it had been her mother who had worked out the practical details and somehow found the money to finance her modestly in London while she completed the studies already begun under her father's admirable guidance in the small West Country town in which she had grown up.

Anna was now in her third year at one of the famous London music colleges, and this time when she had come home on holiday she had been able to report more than academic progress. Already some engagements as soloist with one or two quite important church choirs had come her way. And at the last end-of-term college performance she had attracted outstanding mention from more than one of the London music critics.

"The important thing now is not to rush things," her

6

father had immediately warned her. "No heavy, voice-damaging roles, remember. No temptations to take big money or easy applause just because you have an outstanding voice with genuine brilliance."

"No, Dad, of course not," Anna agreed, with difficulty resisting the impulse to point out that no one was exactly beating a pathway to her front door with offers of star roles.

"That has been the death of many a fine talent in the last two decades," her father went on, developing one of his favourite lines of argument. And, since she had the good sense to know that much of what he said was right, Anna had listened with grave attention to words she had heard many times before.

At twenty-two, she was unusually perceptive about people – even to a certain extent about herself, which is rare at that age. She knew quite well that she had inherited a great deal from both parents and, since they were strikingly unalike in disposition, she was sometimes aware of a conflict within herself. From her father came her musical intelligence, her artistic instinct, her sensitive feeling for beauty and quality; but from her mother came her down-to-earth streak of common sense which told her that facts must be looked in the face, even if they are unpalatable.

Until she went to London she had lived what would nowadays be called a somewhat sheltered life. That is to say, her parents (who would undoubtedly have been classified as old-fashioned by modern theorists) had seen to it that she had a happy, secure, well regulated childhood and came to relative maturity by leisurely and unsensational stages.

No one had concealed from her the fact that life had its grim, dark patches, but no one had encouraged her to dwell on these to the exclusion of everything else. Similarly, although she never doubted her supreme importance to the people who loved her, from an early age she was made fully aware of the needs and claims of other people.

Her transfer to London, where she shared a flat with three other girls, had provided some eye-opening discoveries. But she was adaptable, and she was enormously happy in her work. Without vanity or false modesty, she knew in her inmost heart that she was genuinely gifted and she had never been afraid of hard work. Even this combination, Anna knew, was not sufficient in itself to launch her on a career, but she was optimistic enough to hope that she would also be blessed with the stroke of good luck which is almost invariably one of the essential ingredients of success.

"It's not all just slog and brilliance," her special friend, Judy Edmonds, had said in her second year. "You have to be in the right place at the right time with the right people around – and then you must have luck. Oh, *how* you must have that luck! That's why I myself am quitting. I just don't think I have the right kind of luck."

"You're quitting? Giving up the idea of becoming a singer, you mean?" Anna, who was glimpsing hope on the horizon, was shocked.

"Yes." Judy gave a vigorous little nod of her dark head. "It's not just a question of luck, though that's important enough, as I say. But I'm not really sufficiently gifted, Anna. Yes, I know – " as Anna started to protest – "I have a good voice, I'm musical and I'm quite attractive. It's not enough. There are dozens – hundreds – like me trooping in and out of every music college in the land. The only difference between them and me is that I've faced the fact that only the gifted few earn their

8

living by doing what they really want to do. The others settle for something humdrum but reasonably rewarding."

"Such as?"

"For every singer, actress, artist, writer that this world can absorb, how many really good secretaries do you suppose are needed?"

Anna was silent, digesting this.

"There are few enough of *them*, goodness knows!" Judy went on cheerfully. "I'm facing the fact now that I'll be happier and have more self-respect as a good secretary enjoying music as a hobby than as a not-very-good performer in an overcrowded market. I'm reasonably well educated, I'm nobody's fool, and I have a couple of useful foreign languages. With six or nine months' intensive training I reckon I shall be able to take my pick of several good jobs. That makes more sense to me than struggling on as I am."

"Then it doesn't make sense to you that I *do* intend to struggle on as I am?" Anna said, making a little face.

"Ah, that's different!"

"In what way?"

"I don't quite know." Judy ruffled up her hair consideringly. "For one thing, you have a much finer, more individual voice than I have. It's been developing perfectly beautifully in the last few months. But that's not all. There's something about it – about you, I suppose. Even though you're little more than a student yet, you have the quality that – that transports one. Do you know what I mean?"

"I think I do," Anna said slowly. "I didn't know I had it, though."

"It's something one can't either teach or learn," Judy went on, frowning with the effort to make herself clear. "It carries a sort of uplift and conviction straight from

9

the singer to the listener. Oh, *how* do I explain it? It's like – well, fifty people can sing, 'I know that my Redeemer liveth', and it's all very lovely and fine. Then one more comes along, and suddenly everyone knows that He *does* live. Just like that! Or a singer sings 'I love you – ' in perhaps the most hackneyed operatic phrase, and all at once it carries to everyone in the house the absolute conviction that love is real and might touch any one of us any day."

"Yes, I do know what you mean," Anna confirmed, her tone slightly awed at this suggestion that she might herself possess such a rare gift. "It's a sort of fusing of words and music and instinct and training – and something indefinable as well."

"And something indefinable as well," Judy agreed. "That's what you have, I'm nearly sure. And with hard work and some luck you'll really be something one day. Meanwhile, I intend to be a darn good secretary."

She was, too. In less than a year, she was firmly established with an internationally famous music publishing firm with, as she said, a sufficiently good salary to attend most of the musical performances she wanted to hear.

The two girls remained fast friends, with a warm interest in each other's fortunes, though Judy was not one of the girls who shared a flat with Anna, preferring to live at home with her family in one of the outer suburbs. They lunched together at least twice a week, however, and it was on one of these occasions that Judy supplied the information that Jonathan Keyne was looking for good young talent for an operatic company he planned to take on a tour of Canada, the following spring.

"I don't know the full repertoire," Judy admitted. "But he's bound to include 'Figaro' because Donald Spyres is going and that's one of his principal roles. Why don't you boldly ask to be auditioned for Susanna? He'll be auditioning in about a month's time."

"How do you know all this?" Anna asked eagerly.

"Oh, I keep my ear to the ground," replied Judy airily. Then she grinned and added, "As a matter of fact, I heard Oscar Warrender talking about it."

"You *heard* Oscar Warrender talking about it?" Anna was impressed. "When and where?"

"In the office, yesterday. He was talking to Mr. Prendergast. He does drop in occasionally when he wants a special score or something."

"You secretaries do live it up, don't you?" said Anna with a frankly envious little laugh. "Oscar Warrender and Jonathan Keyne! It's almost too much."

"Jonathan Keyne wasn't actually there. I just heard about him."

"Yes, I know." Anna suddenly smiled reminiscently. "He was on the selection board when I was admitted to the college, you know. I remember him very well. I don't think he was much impressed by me then."

"That's a long time ago," Judy said quickly.

"Yes, it's a long time ago." Anna looked thoughtful. "I wonder what he'd think of me now. I'd like a chance of impressing him! I remember how it riled me that he was so indifferent then."

"Why did it *rile* you?" Judy seized on the word. "Did you feel he was unjust to you?"

"N-no, not that, exactly," Anna admitted. "I suppose the fact is that he's the kind of man one very much *wants* to impress. He's an arresting sort of person. Attractive, authoritative – unusually authoritative for anyone of thirty, or whatever he is. He was talking to the other judges, I remember, when I came in, and they were all laughing. There was an immense gay vitality about him.

And then, when he turned to the business of hearing the next unimportant applicant – who was me – I just felt I was an unwelcome interruption to an enjoyable occasion. It's difficult to build up a big entry on that!"

"It would be quite different now," Judy asserted. "Be sure you write to him before you go away on holiday, and don't hesitate to enclose those last notices you got. Even if you get no further than auditioning for him this time he won't forget you again. And it's useful to establish yourself favourably in the memory of a man like Keyne. He's already wielding a lot of influence in the musical world, and he'll go further still."

"I suppose you're right," agreed Anna, wishing she did not recall with quite such painful clarity the faintly bored way his glance had passed over her as she tremblingly launched into the exacting Handel aria which had been chosen as the test piece.

"Of course I'm right," Judy insisted emphatically. "It's not only that he's such a gifted musician himself. He has a real flair for spotting and developing talent. Warrender said he'd rather have Keyne direct a musical festival than many men twice his age. And Anthea Warrender agreed with him."

"Was she there too in the office? – Warrender's wife. What is she like, close to?" Anna asked curiously.

"Lovely." Judy spoke without reservation. "She looks the complete prima donna nowadays. And yet somehow, if you lived next door, you wouldn't mind going and asking her to take in the laundry for you."

"I would!" declared Anna with conviction. "After all, *he* might answer the door. Think of that!"

They had both laughed immoderately over this idea, and parted in excellent spirits. But before she left London Anna wrote to Jonathan Keyne, explaining that she had heard he was looking for new singers to take part in a Canadian opera tour, and asking for an audition.

With considerable difficulty and the exercise of much self-discipline, she had managed to keep from her parents any hint of her hopes. After all, the chances were that nothing would come of her application, and there was no point in preparing a disappointment for anyone other than herself. There were, alas, already too many insecurely based hopes waiting for extinction in their household.

It was true, as her mother had said, that no experience of repeated rebuffs seemed to dim her father's conviction that one day he would write something which the world would hail as a masterpiece. A minor masterpiece, perhaps, but still something that would give him a modest place in the great hierarchy of those he most loved and admired – the men who had given beautiful music to the world. But the moment when hope was dashed yet again could not possibly be anything but a painful one.

Three days later, when the morning post brought the verdict that yet another of Kenneth Fulroyd's works had proved unacceptable to an indifferent world, Anna was alone with him at the breakfast table. She had known from the flush of eagerness with which he picked up the envelope what he was hoping. And she realised even more poignantly from the tremor of his hands as he read the single sheet what the answer was.

Presently he went on eating his breakfast while she tried, quite fruitlessly, to think of something to say. In the end, it was he who spoke first.

"Well, Anna –" his half nervous little laugh wrung her heart – "I'm afraid it's going to be left to you to bring any musical fame to this family."

"I did hope that, as it was a letter and not a parcel, perhaps the manuscript had been accepted this time," she

13

said gently.

"The same idea struck me. But they say they're returning it under separate cover." He stirred his coffee and looked once more at the few typed lines, as though he might still discover some hidden ray of encouragement.

"Dad, I'm so sorry! Judy always says one has to have luck, as well as all the other qualities. Perhaps – perhaps your luck just isn't in at the moment."

"It's more than *I* am just not 'in' at the moment," replied her father, with more realism than he usually showed. "It's a harsh, unlovely period, Anna. Sometimes I think no one wants beauty and grace and melody any more."

"You don't think," Anna ventured diffidently, "that perhaps you over-estimate the – the scope of what's required today? I mean, your works do require huge casts, and most of them would be terribly difficult to stage, whereas – "

"My dear!" the objection was brushed aside with some amusement. "This is reckoned to be the age of theatrical miracles. Staging should present no problems. Look back a hundred and fifty years and think what composers were demanding then! Rossini, for instance, in his 'Moses', calmly throwing in the crossing of the Red Sea by the Children of Israel, not to mention the destruction of the Egyptian army following them. That's what you might call a difficult theatrical situation, if you like."

Anna was inclined to agree. But she lacked the courage to point out that no one lightly undertook the staging of "Moses" either in these days. Instead, she crossed her arms on the table, smiled encouragingly at her father and said,

"Don't you ever feel moved to try something on a – a less ambitious scale? Say something for piano or organ –

or perhaps chamber music?"

"You talk like your mother." He said that kindly and without condescension, but there was a note of reproof in his tone. "As an artist yourself, you must know that genius – even talent – must express itself in its own way or not at all."

Anna knew it was cowardly of her not to point out immediately that genius – and even talent – undisciplined could often produce no more than a shapeless, self-indulgent piece of mediocrity. But she had not the heart to add sharp argument to his present disappointment.

Instead, she asked suddenly, "What was that lovely thing you were playing in church yesterday evening, when I dropped in after choir practice?"

"Yesterday evening?" He frowned consideringly. "Some Bach, I expect."

"No, no, nothing eighteenth century. It was something I didn't know at all. Tommy Bream came in just about then to retrieve his copy of the anthem, which he'd left behind as usual."

"*That*?" her father laughed. "I was just improvising."

"Improvising? You mean you composed it? But it was lovely. So simple and noble. What was it meant to be?"

"I have no idea." Her father got up, dismissing the matter as irrelevant. "I must go or I shall be late for school. Don't tell your mother yet about this disappointment. She takes these things to heart, because she always believes that this time I'll make a success."

He picked up a pile of music with a sigh and went on his way to school, leaving his daughter to reflect with some astonishment that two people could live together in harmony for years and yet not really know the inmost thoughts of each other.

"He doesn't know even now how Mother really feels

15

about his work," she thought with affectionate impatience. "Nor does he know his own talents! That was a lovely air – and he hasn't even retained it in his memory. Besides, if he did, he'd just smother it under the weight of some huge musical structure. He understands so much about music, bless him – but not the appeal of divine simplicity."

She presumed that he broke the news of his disappointment to her mother, and that her mother went through the motions of being surprised and indignant. But nothing else was said about the rejected masterpiece. There were a few rather quiet, somewhat dejected days, and then Anna felt sure that her father began to busy himself again on new plans.

When he said good-bye to her at the end of the holiday, however, he added some unexpected words.

"Perhaps some people are born to realise their ambitions only in their children, Anna. Good luck, my dear, in all your hopes and plans. If you succeed, I shan't mind my own failures."

She was considerably moved and also, not unnaturally, overwhelmed by a deep sense of responsibility. It was one thing to live with one's own hopes and fears; it was a sobering thought to feel that someone else's ambitions were tied to them too.

More than ever was she glad that she had not told her parents about her approach to Jonathan Keyne. After all, he might not even bother to answer her.

His reply was waiting, however, when she returned to London. And, as she stood in the silent, sun-filled flat – it was the afternoon and the other girls were all out – the envelope shook in her hand. Just as her father's hand had shaken, she remembered, as he opened the letter which contained the answer to *his* hopes.

Her letter also consisted of no more than a few lines. But those lines bade her come and audition for Jonathan Keyne at the Carrington Studios on the following Monday.

Anna was immediately thrown into a fever of excitement and hope, cooled only by the fear that her holiday might have put her slightly out of practice. But then, she remembered, her father had insisted that she worked with him, even on holiday, and she knew his advice and guidance had been on excellent lines. She longed to share her good news with someone. But Judy was also on holiday until the following Monday, and the girls with whom she shared the flat would display little interest, even when they did come in.

They wished her well, but two of them were air hostesses with very varied interests of their own, and the third one, Carrie – though a charming and good-natured girl – had long ago been slightly deafened and rendered totally insensitive to any real music by the fact that the store where she worked assaulted the ears of staff and customers alike with piped music all day long.

Finally, Anna telephoned to her singing teacher, Elsa Marburger, who had done so much to launch that successful contralto Gail Rostall on her career. Madame Marburger received the news of the Jonathan Keyne audition with a certain degree of cautious congratulation, and said that naturally Anna would need to come for some special coaching during the few days left to them.

"You are not ready for leading roles, of course," she said firmly, when Anna presented herself the following morning. "But some understudy work and one or two minor roles would be excellent experience at this stage."

"I thought," stated Anna boldly, "of asking to be considered for Susanna. I believe they're doing 'Fig-' "

"Susanna," said Madame Marburger rather coldly, "is not a minor role. It is one of the most difficult and subtle in the whole operatic repertoire."

"Then perhaps Barbarina?" suggested Anna, somewhat diminished. "And as I've already done a lot of work on Susanna in the studio, possibly I might have a chance of understudying the part on this tour."

"That," her teacher agreed, "would be more realistic. For the rest, since you don't know what else is being included, we will concentrate on items which show off your voice to the best advantage."

This, then, they proceeded to do. And by the weekend the seesaw of Anna's hopes and fears had steadied itself sufficiently for her to believe that she would at least do herself justice when the great moment came. Beyond that, everything would depend on the stiffness of the competition, of course. For she could not doubt that there would be many lyric sopranos besides herself who would covet the chance of touring Canada under the directorship of Jonathan Keyne.

Some of them were already gathered there in the waiting-room when she arrived on Monday afternoon at the Carrington Studios – a chill and shabby place with splendid acoustics. As one after the other was called into the large adjoining studio Anna had time to steady her nerves. But when the only one left besides herself was summoned, she found that there was still time to grow panicky again.

Faintly she could hear sounds of the other girl singing, and each time there was a pause Anna felt her heart thump more heavily. Eventually, after a somewhat longer pause, there was the sound of a closing door. And a few moments later the rather weary-looking accompanist came to the waiting-room door and said, "Are you Miss

Fulroyd? You're the last, then."

And Anna walked into the big studio.

Jonathan Keyne was sitting at a table, with scores and papers spread out in front of him. But he looked up as Anna came in, gave her a penetrating glance and said immediately, "Didn't you audition for me once before, Miss Fulroyd?"

"Not professionally." She was gratified beyond measure that apparently she *had* registered with him after all! "You were on the board when I was auditioned for entry to St. Cecilia's College."

"I remember." She saw that he did too. "You sang a Handel aria. Rather well, if I remember rightly."

"Did I? – sing it well, I mean."

"Certainly. Didn't you think so?" He looked amused. "Most students today tend to have a higher opinion of their work than the judges do."

Anna laughed, and suddenly felt much more at ease.

"I think I was too nervous to know how I sang it," she confessed. "But I certainly thought – "

She stopped, shocked at what she had been about to say, and he asked curiously, "What did you think?"

"I – I had the impression that you didn't think much of it. You looked rather bored, to tell the truth."

"Did I really? How very remiss of me. Examiners should never look bored. Should they, Peter?" He grinned suddenly at the accompanist.

"Depends how many others they've had to hear that day," replied the accompanist with a thin smile. "What are you going to sing, Miss Fuller?"

"The name is Fulroyd. Anna Fulroyd," said Jonathan Keyne distinctly. And then she really did believe that she had made some sort of impact on him three years ago.

She sang Susanna's last act aria. And because she was

19

now relaxed and somehow elated she sang it well. Neither Jonathan Keyne nor the accompanist could be accused of looking bored this time. And at the end, Jonathan Keyne asked, "Do you sing the role?"

"I have studied it fully. I've never had an opportunity to sing it on the stage."

"And Pamina? Do you do that too?"

She felt Madame Marburger would deplore her making any real claim to "doing" Pamina. But, still with a feeling of gay, warm confidence, she said once more – and quite truly – that she knew the role fully but had not had an opportunity to sing it on stage.

"Sing me '*Ach, ich fuhls*'," he said peremptorily.

She did so, and noticed that he smiled slightly with what looked like pleasure as she negotiated the difficult high passages with skill and real beauty.

"Who is your teacher?" he enquired when she had finished.

"Elsa Marburger."

"Ah-ha – " he laughed comprehendingly – "that explains the genuine Mozart style. Keeps you pretty firmly on the eighteenth century classics, I imagine?"

"Well, a good deal of the time – yes."

"Any indulgent excursions into the romantics?" And then, as Anna hesitated – "I ask that because of course we are including one or two of the most popular works. 'Boheme', for instance. Do you sing Musetta?"

"I have sung the famous Waltz Song, of course. But – "

"Sing it for me now."

"I'm afraid I haven't the music – "

"Doesn't matter. Peter can do it in his sleep. Can't you, Peter?"

Peter said he could. But before he could start, Jonathan Keyne leant forward suddenly with his arms on the table, and fixed Anna with an almost commanding glance.

"Think about it for a moment," he advised her. "Remember the exact situation. And, whatever you do, don't be condescending about it or superficial. Use some of that Mozart training, if you like. For that poor, misused little song of Musetta's is actually one of the cleverest, most stylish things ever written."

She stood for a moment or two with her head bent. Then she looked up and smiled across at the accompanist, and he played the opening bars. From somewhere deep down in her musical consciousness Anna drew on her instinctive sense of style, and because of what Jonathan Keyne had just said to her she realised, for the first time, that Musetta was not a brazen hussy, but just a gay, rather touching *fille de joie*. No more than a transient bubble on the stream of the bohemian life of Paris, yet sealed for ever in her moment of immortality by the ravishing tune which Puccini had given to her.

Neither of the men said anything for a moment or two after she had finished. Then Jonathan Keyne, his arms crossed in a contented sort of way, leaned back in his chair and smiled at the accompanist.

"Feel better, Peter?" was the odd thing he said.

"Much better," replied Peter. "It takes some of the sour taste out of one's mouth."

Anna looked, amused and enquiring, from one man to the other. And Jonathan Keyne said, "Peter is a fanatical Puccini enthusiast, which is hard on him because he has to hear his favourite music half murdered over and over again."

"It's virtually indestructible, you see," Peter explained suddenly. "And so every fool makes some sort of rotten shot at it. This Waltz Song of Musetta's, for instance. About twenty years ago someone had the fatuous idea of giving it to a luscious dramatic soprano, who shall be nameless. She was enormously successful, of course, because the public always loves to hear its favourite tunes bawled at the top of someone's voice. But she transformed the character into a sort of 'madam' in a bawdy house."

"Since then," went on Keyne as Peter lapsed into gloomy silence, "most aspiring Musettas play it for noise and bouncing vitality, and they get the kind of cheers usually reserved for successful footballers. It hurts poor old Peter every time. My guess is that he'd like to kiss you here and now for restoring Musetta to her right interpretation."

"I'd like Warrender to hear her," said Peter, without offering to make good the suggested kiss.

"So would I," agreed Jonathan Keyne unexpectedly. "Miss Fulroyd, let's say frankly that we are exceedingly interested in you. But of course there is a good deal more material to consider and not all that number of vacancies to fill. Oscar Warrender has agreed to sit in on the final selection. I'd like you to be one of those he hears. Leave your phone number, will you? and we'll let you know about dates and times."

She could not conceal her joy, and he laughed warningly.

"You're not actually engaged yet, you know. But we're very glad indeed that you came along."

She was glad too! So glad that she went out of the Carrington Studios in a haze of bliss, and walked for nearly ten minutes without looking where she was going before she realised that she was very near Judy's office and that it was just about her usual time for leaving.

Anna walked up and down on the pavement, finding it difficult not to smile beatifically at everyone she passed.

She kept her eye on the imposing entrance to Judy's office, and was presently rewarded by the sight of none other than Oscar Warrender emerging from the building and pausing for a moment on the pavement to hail a taxi.

There was something almost symbolical about the brief encounter at this particular time, Anna could not help thinking, and she had to suppress a crazy impulse to go up to him and say, "You don't know it, but I'm going to sing for you in a few days' time."

Naturally, she retained sufficient sanity to restrain herself from doing any such thing, and just as he drove off in his taxi Judy came running down the few steps from the office.

"Hel*lo*!" She was delighted to see Anna and caught her affectionately by the arm. "Did you see who grandly preceded me down those humdrum steps?"

"I did. And was suitably impressed," Anna assured her. "As I knew it was your first day back from holiday and I've just come from auditioning for Jonathan Keyne–"

"You *have*? What happened?"

"It went very well, and I'm daring to be hopeful. He asked me to leave my phone number so that he could–"

"Oh, no!" Judy gave a wail of dismay.

"Why not?" Anna looked startled.

"Oh, you know the old gag – 'Don't phone us, we'll phone you.' It just means, 'Don't bother us any more because you're never going to hear from us again.'"

"Well, this didn't mean anything of the kind," Anna asserted firmly. "Just let me finish what I was going to say."

Upon which she proceeded to give Judy a detailed account of her afternoon, and as she finished the saga over a cup of tea in a nearby café, Judy agreed whole-heartedly that hope was more than justified.

"Mind, the next few days are going to be pretty tough," she warned. "Your heart will be in your throat every time the phone bell rings."

"I'll live through it," Anna declared philosophically.

And live through it she did, of course, though Judy had been perfectly correct in saying that the real nerve-test would be each time the telephone rang – which it did pretty frequently in a flat which housed four not unattractive girls.

It was just a week after her original audition, about nine o'clock in the morning, when the telephone bell rang yet again and Carrie, who reached it first, called, "For you, Anna. You'd better hurry. Sounds like a long-distance call."

It couldn't possibly be a long-distance call, Anna felt sure, as she ran into the hall. No one ever telephoned from home except in the evening, when the reduced rate made a long conversation seem less extravagant. It must be – it *must* be –

She seized up the receiver and in a not entirely steady voice said, "Yes? – this is Anna Fulroyd."

"Anna – " to her astonishment it was her father, and something – perhaps the distance – seemed to lend a sort of agitation to his tone. "Anna, is that you?"

"Yes – yes, of course it is. What is it, Dad? Is something wrong?"

The voice at the other end faded in a maddening way, and all she could hear was something about – "Your mother – she didn't want you to be worried, but I think you should know – "

"*What* should I know?" Indescribable chill seized Anna, with a force she could not understand. "I can't hear very well. Say that again, Dad. What was that about Mother?"

"– into hospital at eight o'clock this morning – " Then suddenly the line cleared almost miraculously and her father's worried voice said almost in her ear, "She hasn't been herself for some time. You probably noticed when you were here, but she insisted you shouldn't be worried."

"But what *is* it? You haven't said what is really wrong."

"What's that, dear?" Apparently the wretched line had faded at his end now. "What is it, did you say? We don't know. That's why the doctor rushed her into hospital. They're operating this afternoon. It could be just exploratory, but it might be much more serious, because – "A sort of rattling intervened at this point and all Anna heard after that was – "confounded line – but I'll phone later this afternoon – "

Then the line went dead and Anna was left standing there in the hall of the flat, miles and miles and miles away from any source of information, just staring at the silent receiver in her hand, as though it were a snake which had suddenly risen in her hitherto happy path.

"Coffee's ready," called Carrie cheerfully from the kitchen.

"I'll join you in a minute." Anna came to the kitchen door to explain. "That was an urgent call from home. My mother's had to go to hospital. I couldn't hear any details because the line was bad. I must call back and ask my father – "

But before she could do that the telephone bell rang again.

"There he is! He must have re-connected from his end." And she rushed to pick up the receiver once more.

It was not her father this time, however. It was Jonathan Keyne's pleasant but slightly peremptory voice which said, "I should like to speak to Miss Anna Fulroyd, please."

"I'm speaking, Mr. Keyne."

"Oh – " he sounded amused but not at all displeased at being recognised – "this is very short notice, I know, but would you come along to the Carrington Studios again this afternoon at three?"

"This – this afternoon would be difficult," she stammered, her father's worried, disjointed sentences still ringing in her ears. "You see – "

"It's important, Miss Fulroyd. Could be very important to you." She wondered if she only fancied a slight cooling of the tone. "Warrender has an hour or two available, and we're going to do some final sorting out. I'd be sorry for him not to hear you."

She would be sorry too! And somehow the wording rather implied that it would be now or never.

"When did you say? I'll be there," Anna promised desperately.

"Three o'clock. Carrington Studios as before." And then he rang off.

"I must get hold of Dad and explain," muttered Anna, beginning to dial frantically. She heard the click of the connection and then the ringing of the bell the other end. But although she let it ring for quite a long time there was no reply, and she guessed that her father had probably been telephoning direct from the hospital.

She tried once more through the operator, just to make sure, but with the same result. And finally there was nothing to do but replace the receiver and go to join Carrie in the kitchen.

Carrie, who had the day off and was luxuriating in an unusually leisurely breakfast, looked up immediately as she came in.

"Any further news?" she enquired sympathetically.

"No. I can't get through. Dad couldn't have been phoning from home. He said he would call again this afternoon after – after the operation. But, Carrie, I just have to go out. It's an audition – just about the most important audition that's ever come my way. What can I *do*?"

"Leave the number of wherever you're going with me, of course," replied Carrie, who was bright enough when not being stupefied by the row in her store. "I happen to have the day off."

"Oh, but weren't you going out?"

"I was. But it's nothing important. Just a movie with Len, and it's time I said 'no' to him occasionally. He's getting a bit above himself anyway. Leave the number with me, and when your dad rings I'll tell him where to find you. I suppose there will be some arrangement where you can take a call at this place where you're going?"

"There must be, of course. Oh, Carrie, you're an angel!" And, almost sick with relief, Anna began to search through the directory for the telephone number of the Carrington Studios. "Yes, here it is." She scribbled it down hastily. "And I'll be back the first moment I can get away. I may well be back even before Dad phones with – with better news – "

And then suddenly she could say no more. For suppose it were *not* better news – suppose something should happen to her mother –

But nothing could happen, of course! Nothing – irrevocable, that was. Not to her mother, who was the very personification of security and normality. It was unthinkable. Particularly just now, when everything promised to go as she and her parents had hoped and planned for so long.

"I ought to have realised something was wrong, when I was at home," she thought remorsefully. "I did think once or twice that she was preoccupied, almost *sad*. Why didn't I ask her then? I was just too selfishly intent on my own affairs. And what, for heaven's sake, do they matter if anything really happened to Mother?"

But they did matter, of course. They mattered terribly. Everything she had done for the last few years had been geared to reaching the sort of goal which was to be dangled before her that very afternoon. It was no good feeling guilty because the thought of that vital audition kept on blotting out everything else. There was no point in going to that all-important audition with less than total concentration on doing her best. Even her mother, lying ill in hospital, waiting to be taken to the operating theatre –

Desperately, she switched her thoughts from the possibilities implicit in that reflection and willed herself to be calm as she went to her morning lesson with her teacher.

Madame Marburger, characteristically, was sympathetic about Anna's personal trouble, but very bracing about the necessity of concentrating all her thoughts and energies on the testing afternoon.

"An artist's life is full of this sort of crisis," she told Anna. "You are just having to learn rather early that even the deepest personal feelings have to take second place to a professional emergency. You could do nothing for your mother if you were there, and you owe it to her, and her sacrifices on your behalf, to do your best this afternoon."

This was sound, if ruthless, common sense, of course. And, having telephoned to Carrie and ascertained that no message had yet come through, Anna went to the studio that afternoon at least outwardly calm and relaxed.

It was not difficult to arrange that she should be called if anyone telephoned for her. "Though I couldn't interrupt, of course, if you were actually in the studio," the man in charge warned her. "Mr. Warrender's auditioning this afternoon, as you probably know, and it's a great deal more than any of us would dare to interrupt *him*. But so long as you're still in the waiting room it will be all right."

Anna thanked him and went to the waiting room, where she found about half a dozen other singers in varying degrees of tension. None of them had been there at her previous audition and she guessed that some pretty ruthless weeding out had been done during the past week.

After what the doorman had said she was prepared to find Oscar Warrender autocratic and disagreeable. But when her turn came and she was summoned to the studio, he treated her with the utmost courtesy. His invariable rule, had she but known it, when he wished to get the best out of someone, although, in the words of one disgruntled prima donna, "if he wished he could also be a monster."

At this time Oscar Warrender was well past his first youth but still a strikingly handsome man, with an air of command so natural to him that one would have said he was unaware that most heads turned when he passed. One would, however, have been wrong in this. Warrender had served his art faithfully all his life, with devotion and integrity, love and sheer hard work and, as he sometimes said himself, he would have been a fool not to savour the just rewards which had crowned his later years.

"Unless you specially wish to sing something else, Miss Fulroyd," he told Anna without preamble, "I should like to hear the three arias you sang for Mr. Keyne last week."

So Anna sang the two Mozart arias, but before she could go on to Musetta's Waltz Song he stopped her and talked to her for a few minutes about the phrasing in the

Pamina aria, suggesting one or two modifications, but with an air of talking to someone whose own views might not be negligible. Indeed, when she ventured to query something he suggested, he said,

"You feel it should go that way? Try it, then, and let me hear it again." And, after she had done so – "Yes, it's not impossible. If you feel comfortable with it that way, keep to it. Elsa Marburger is your teacher, I believe?"

"Yes, Mr. Warrender."

"You do her credit," was the brief reply, and Anna thought she knew how people must feel when they were knighted.

For a moment or two he and Jonathan Keyne conferred together in low tones, while Anna tried to look innocently unknowing, though she thought she heard Oscar Warrender say, "The girl this morning had more experience, of course."

Jonathan Keyne did not let that go unchallenged, she noticed, and Warrender said, "Yes, yes, I grant you that," before he turned back to Anna and asked for Musetta's song.

Ever since she had sung this for Jonathan Keyne a week ago she had been thinking about what he had said, and how the part of Musetta called for charm and sparkle and a touch of pathos, all within a stylish, completely unvulgar framework. This was how she sang it now. And she was rewarded by seeing Warrender's rare, extremely attractive smile as he turned to Keyne and said,

"Yes, I see what you mean."

This one remark was not amplified at the moment, and Anna was asked to return to the waiting room, but told not to leave as she would be required again.

She went back, aware of an indescribable sensation of warm, calm satisfaction. She knew she had done very well, and she was certain that both those influential men had been well impressed by her. It was difficult not to feel that the contract was virtually hers, and it was equally difficult not to feel elated and happy beyond measure.

Only the sudden recollection of her mother's condition shocked her back into a sense of fear and anxiety. And just because her personal qualms were so entirely at rest the return of her fears for her mother became all the more poignant. She found suddenly that she was trembling uncontrollably, so that the young man sitting nearest to her asked anxiously, "Was Warrender beastly?"

"No! Far from it. He was very fair and – and courteous. It's something else – "

She broke off abruptly as the doorman looked in and, catching sight of her, beckoned.

For a moment she found she could hardly stand up. Then she forced herself to her feet and followed him out into the corridor, where he indicated a telephone, set in an angle in the wall.

"You'd better take it there. It's the nearest extension. I've told the gentleman to hold on for a minute or two while I fetched you."

Anna murmured a word of thanks, clutched the receiver in a cold hand and, having cleared her throat twice, managed to say hoarsely, "This is Anna speaking."

"Anna dear – " her father's tone was perfectly clear this time and singularly calm after the agitation of that morning call – "can you catch the next train down? The six o'clock, if possible. You'd better be here. The news is worse than we feared."

"Mother – " her tongue felt thick and stiff in her mouth. "Yes, I'll come, of course. If I hurry, I can manage the six o'clock. Tell me, Dad, how – how bad is it?"

"Of course, there's always hope – remember that. But

–" his tone did waver a little then – "I think if you want to see her you must hurry."

"I'm coming," Anna said. "I'm coming this very minute." And she put down the telephone and began to run down the corridor. As she did so she almost cannoned into Jonathan Keyne, who caught her by the arm and exclaimed laughingly,

"Here, where are you running? We want you back in the studio."

"I can't come." She tried to wrench her arm away, and was astonished even then by the strength with which he held her. "I can't come. I'm going home."

"You're not, you know." He spoke with cool, almost grim, determination. "You're coming back with me to hear the terms of your contract."

"Contract?" She stared at him for a moment as though she hardly understood the meaning of the word. "Contract? – Oh, I don't care about any contract now! Leave me *alone*!"

And she tore herself free and sped along the corridor, while Jonathan Keyne looked after her, his expression blank with astonishment until slowly a dark flush of intense anger spread over his face.

CHAPTER TWO

ANNA never forgot the misery of that long journey home. Even years afterwards she could hardly bear to think of it, with its weight of crushing anxiety making everything seem grey and vague around her, all her jangled nerves concentrating on the sharpness of her fear about her mother.

When she had rushed from the studio, leaving an angry and astonished Jonathan Keyne behind her, she had been fortunate enough to pick up a taxi immediately outside. But the rush-hour traffic was already building up and there were several maddening delays before she finally erupted into the flat, explained briefly to Carrie about the emergency, threw a few necessary things into a case and hurried off again.

Almost as she went, Carrie thought to call after her, "How did the audition go?"

"All right, I think. But it doesn't matter now. That's all over," Anna replied, and then she was on her way to the station, where she arrived just in time to catch the six o'clock train.

But Carrie's last-minute enquiry did serve to switch her thoughts for a few minutes to her own affairs and the unfortunate way in which she had parted from Jonathan Keyne.

"He must have thought me mad," she reflected unhappily. "Well, I suppose I was, just for a few minutes. I can't remember what I actually said. I don't think I explained at all – just pulled my arm away and shouted to him to leave me alone. How awful! As though I wanted to insult him. But it doesn't matter now. Nothing matters except that Mother might be dying."

The journey took two hours and a half, and it rained almost all the way, sinking Anna's spirits to an even lower ebb if that were possible. When the train finally stopped at her station the rain was coming down in torrents, and a vicious wind was sweeping the open platform.

There was no sign of her father, which increased her alarm, because he knew that she had more than a mile to walk from the station unless the local taxi was sent to meet her, and obviously he had been too much concerned even to remember this necessary arrangement.

The only vehicle standing outside the station was a handsome black car which, in a less confused moment, Anna would have identified as belonging to one or other of the Delawneys, the "local millionaires" as they were usually referred to – half scornfully, half admiringly – by residents of long standing in the district.

As she stood there, undecided and shivering slightly under the onslaught of wind and rain, a clear, pleasant voice behind her said, "Can I give you a lift? It's not exactly walking weather, is it?" and Anna turned to see that it was the Delawney son, Roderick, who was reputed to be a partner in some fantastically prosperous enterprise in the City of London, but who quite frequently visited the family home.

"Thank you very much. I – "

"It's Miss Fulroyd, isn't it?" he interrupted. "And your father is the local organist – right? I was telling my sister that she ought to get in touch with him about this festival lark she's arranging. Jump in." He held open the door and greeted the chauffeur with, "Hello, Jenkins. You slip into the back. I'll drive and Miss Fulroyd will come in front with me."

Within moments he had arranged things as he wished, and as they drove off, he said to Anna, "I'll drop you right at your door. It's the white house, isn't it, at the end – "

"Please – " she managed to arrest the spate of good-humoured arrangements – "could you drop me at the Cottage Hospital, if that isn't out of your way?"

"Of course." He glanced at her, as though he took in for the first time her strained and preoccupied air. "I'm sorry. Are you visiting someone there?"

"It's – my mother. She had an operation this afternoon. My father phoned to fetch me from London."

"Oh, that's tough!" He sounded so genuinely concerned that her chilled heart warmed gratefully to him. "Is there anything I can do? Wait for you and take you home afterwards, perhaps?"

"No, thank you. But how – how very kind of you." Her voice shook uncontrollably because his uninhibited willingness to be of help brought a lump into her throat. "I expect my father will be there. I think he's been there all day. It's – it's serious, you see."

"There's almost no limit to what doctors can do these days." He removed one strong brown hand from the wheel to clasp it reassuringly over hers. "Don't give up hope."

"N-no, of course not." She was ashamed that a tear escaped, rolled down her cheek and fell on his hand. "It's just that it's all so sudden and unbelievable. Mother was – is, I mean – the most stable, secure force in our family and –"

"I know. It's the same with us. In the nicest way possible, my mother wears the trousers too," he agreed.

This was not, of course, at all the way Anna would have

described her mother's position in their family. But his sympathy and identification with her troubles were so complete that she accepted his reassurance as it was meant. And at that moment the car turned into the small forecourt in front of the hospital.

"Wait here, Jenkins, for a minute or two. I'm going in with Miss Fulroyd to see she's all right."

"Oh, you mustn't really! My father – "

"If he's there, that will be fine. But I just want to make sure you're not left there on your own."

It was impossible to press the argument further. In any case, in some indefinable way, she was glad of his bracing company as they entered the hospital. And even more so when she found that her voice completely deserted her when it came to asking for the vital information at the enquiry desk.

As she stood there, wordlessly twisting her damp gloves, he took over without hesitation, addressing the man at the desk with that characteristic air of pleasant authority.

"We've come to enquire about a Mrs. Fulroyd, admitted this morning for an emergency operation. This is her daughter from London and – " he hesitated only a fraction of a second – "I'm a friend of the family. Would you know if Mr. Fulroyd is still in the building?"

"Yes." It was apparently not necessary for the well-informed doorman even to consult his records. "Mrs. Fulroyd had her operation this afternoon and is as well as can be expected. Mr. Fulroyd is in the waiting-room along the corridor there. Third door on the left."

"Fine." Young Delawney turned to Anna. "Would you like me to come with you?"

She shook her head. Then she steadied her trembling lips and managed to say, "You've already been so terribly kind. I can never thank you enough – " she swallowed and then just said again, " – so terribly kind."

"A pleasure," he assured her. "Keep up your heart. I'll make enquiries tomorrow, if I may." Then he patted her shoulder and went out of the hospital into the rain once more.

To her surprise, the man at the enquiry desk looked after him and said curiously, "That was young Mr. Delawney, wasn't it? They're good friends of this hospital. Given a thumping cheque towards the new wing. And their money's as good as anyone else's, that's what I say, however recently they came by it. – Third door on the left, and don't mind if your father's a bit upset, Miss Fulroyd. He's had an anxious time, but things are a little better now, I've heard."

"Oh, thank you!" Anna gave him a pale smile and went quickly in search of her father, whom she found in the room indicated, sitting huddled up in an armchair, with an untasted cup of coffee on a table in front of him.

"Dad – " She was beside him, her arms comfortingly round him almost before he knew she was in the room. And when she felt his trembling hand clutching her arm she realised that to anyone as sensitive and vulnerable as her father – anyone who had been in a sense protected for years by her mother – the shocks and horror of the last twenty-four hours must have been almost stupefying.

"It's all right, I'm here. And they say things are a little better – "

"Who says so?" he demanded immediately.

"The – the man at the enquiry desk."

"*He* wouldn't know," exclaimed her father almost querulously.

"He wouldn't presume to say it on his own initiative," she countered bravely. "But tell me all about it, dear.

37

Nothing is going to be so bad now we're together. Drink your coffee. Why – " she touched the side of the cup – "it's quite cold. I'm going to see if I can get some more."

"I don't want any," he said dispiritedly.

"Well, I do. And you must keep me company." She looked round and, seeing a bell, ventured to ring it, whereupon a pleasant, cheerful-looking ward maid immediately presented herself and, before Anna could address her, exclaimed,

"Now, Mr. Fulroyd, you haven't drunk that nice coffee I brought you, and you need something to pick you up after all the worry you've been through."

"If you could most kindly bring us two more cups, I'll see that he drinks his," Anna promised with a slight smile. "I'm his daughter. I'll look after him now."

"Now, isn't that better, Mr. Fulroyd?" The young woman looked approvingly from Anna to her father. "He's been on his own all day, you know," she added in parenthesis to Anna, a little as though her father were a small child and would not know what was being said. "But I keep on telling him the worst is over."

"She doesn't know – any more than the man at the desk does," Anna's father muttered to her irritably. But the young woman evidently had sharp ears, because she replied, without a trace of offence,

"Oh, yes, I do. I mayn't be a qualified nurse, but I haven't been around this hospital for ten years without learning a thing or two. You couldn't have had a better surgeon than Mr. Coombes. He's almost never been known to lose a patient, which is more than some of them can say. And if they say your wife's as well as can be expected that may not mean an awful lot, but it does mean she's alive, and while there's life there's hope. So I'll fetch you some more coffee, and this time you must drink it, if only to please your daughter who's come all this way to be with you."

She went away, and Anna hugged her father again and said, "Can you tell me something about it now, Dad? I don't even know what's the matter with Mother."

"Didn't I tell you on the phone?" He passed a hand distractedly across his forehead. "It's her heart. I thought I told you. That's why she's been finding everything such an effort lately."

"Her heart? Do you mean she's had heart surgery?" Anna, who like most of us had the very vaguest idea of how her heart or anyone else's worked, found it hard to imagine just what even the cleverest of surgeons might have been able to do if that most vital organ gave serious trouble. And, to tell the truth, her father seemed to know very little more than she did.

He tried to explain, so far as he himself had understood, but it all sounded rather strange and improbable to Anna. So she gave up questioning him and, when the coffee and some thick but most welcome sandwiches were brought, she concentrated on being just generally encouraging and hopeful.

She realised, from the pleasure with which he ate his sandwiches, that probably he had had little to eat all day. And only when the meal was finished did she venture to say timidly, "I suppose there's no question of seeing Mother this evening?"

He shook his head.

"They said not until tomorow and perhaps not then. She mustn't have the slightest excitement or fatigue. I only stayed on here because I guessed you would come straight to the hospital and – " He stopped suddenly and gazed at her remorsefully. "Why, I never sent the taxi for you! and it's a terrible evening." He looked at the rain which was still running down the window pane. "How did you get here, my dear? You must have got soaked." And he ran an affectionate hand down her coat sleeve.

"No, no. As you see, I'm quite dry. Except for my gloves, which I dropped in a puddle." She smiled reassuringly at him. "Young Mr. Delawney gave me a lift. Wasn't it kind of him?"

"Young Mr. Delawney?" Her father frowned consideringly. "Do you mean one of the Coppershaw Delawneys?"

"Yes, of course. There aren't any others besides the ones who live at Coppershaw Grange, are there?"

"No. I just thought – How did you come to know him, Anna? Your mother and I don't exactly move in that circle."

"I wasn't moving in his circle." Anna gave a laugh of genuine amusement, which she would not have thought possible half an hour ago. "I was just standing in the wind and rain at the station, and his car was waiting for him and he offered to give me a lift home. I explained about Mother, and he brought me to the hospital. He couldn't have been kinder. He knew who I was, it seems. He knew about you too."

"How do you mean? – he knew about me."

"Well, he asked wasn't I Miss Fulroyd and wasn't my father the organist? Oh, and he said something about telling his sister to get in touch with you about some festival she's organising. What is that, Dad, do you know?"

"Oh, one of those slightly pretentious social affairs, I imagine." Her father smiled faintly, with that touch of scornful indulgence which the professional is rather apt to display towards the wealthy amateur who chooses to dabble in the arts. "I believe the daughter – and possibly

40

Mrs. Delawney too – have some idea of acting as patrons of the arts. All rather amateur, I expect. A few concerts here and there, and some chamber music in the big drawing-room. I believe someone said something about turning the old tithe barn into a theatre, and no doubt there'll be a lot of dressing up. I didn't take it very seriously."

"But it might be rather an attractive plan," protested Anna. "It might be extended to something in the church – and so on. I think it's rather fine of the Delawneys to want to spend some of their money that way. Why not?"

"No reason at all." Suddenly her father smothered an almost irrepressible yawn. "It just didn't strike me as particularly serious. Anna, if there's no point in our staying here any longer – "

"I know! It's time you were home. You must be dead beat. Stay here, dear, and I'll go and see if I can get any more news. And then we'll go home. I think it's stopped raining now."

Presently she managed to find the Night Sister who, though sympathetic, could supply little more information.

"It would be wrong to say she is anything but critically ill, Miss Fulroyd, but she *is* as well as can be expected. In fact, rather better than we dared to hope a few hours ago. It's largely a question now of how well her naturally good constitution can take the strain."

"Would there be any point in our staying on here during the night?" Anna asked.

"None whatever. Even if we had facilities for keeping you, which we haven't. Since you live near and are, I think, on the phone – ?" she paused and Anna nodded – "my advice would be for you to take your father home and try to get him to rest. He's a pretty highly-strung person, isn't he?"

"I'm afraid he is. My mother was always the strong,

41

self-reliant one."

"I guessed as much. Well, get him home and to bed if you can, Miss Fulroyd. Otherwise you'll have another patient on your hands. And you're both going to need a lot of nervous energy during the next week or two, however well your mother does."

So Anna thanked her and went back to the waiting-room, to find her father already anxiously pacing the corridor, convinced that her short absence somehow meant bad news.

"Nothing of the kind, Dad," she reassured him firmly. "On the contrary, the Night Sister says she's better than they'd dared to hope a few hours ago, and that you and I had better go home and get a good night's rest, as we shall need to be well and strong to look after Mother when she's starting the long road back to recovery."

If this was a rather shameless paraphrase of what had actually been said Anna did not trouble her conscience about that. She was just unspeakably relieved to see the way her father's poor, tired face cleared, and how even a little dash of colour came back into his cheeks. He made no further protest and, with his arm linked in hers, walked the short distance to their house with more reassurance and purpose than he had shown since she found him sitting in the waiting room with the cold coffee.

Anna realised that she was at that moment applying the same protective technique to her father which her mother had used during most of her married life. Whether this were wise or not she did not know. But unquestionably he responded to the familiar treatment, and she guessed that during the immediate future she would simply have to replace her mother, so far as her father was concerned.

This indeed proved to be the pattern of her new life.

Contrary to all the early fears, Mrs. Fulroyd continued to hold her own, though there were, of course, setbacks which plunged Anna and her father into fresh terror and near-despair. Then slowly, slowly she began to improve, though she still hovered perilously on the danger list.

"Even when she does eventually go home, she's going to need a very long convalescence," the surgeon explained to Anna. "No exertion, no worry for the next six months at least. What are the arrangements at home? Can she have complete rest there?"

"Yes, of course." Anna made the decision without a moment's hesitation. "I've been in London studying for the last two or three years. But there's no reason why I shouldn't come home now and take over."

"What were you studying?" Mr. Coombes enquired.

"Singing." Anna spoke almost curtly, because when she actually came to speak of her own affairs all her shattered hopes and plans rose up to reproach her. But what else could she do?

"Singing?" The great man smiled indulgently. "Oh, well, I suppose you can take that up again at any time."

"I expect so," agreed Anna drily. For what was the good of trying to explain to a dedicated surgeon that a dedicated artist also had a long, difficult apprenticeship, and that to interrupt things at the wrong moment could spell disaster and eventual failure?

"It's just a question of getting one's priorities right," Anna told herself, swallowing a sudden lump in her throat. "Mother must come first, of course. She's given a lifetime of care to Dad and me. I'd be a poor sort of creature if I grudged her six months or a year of my love and care now."

Strangely enough, even her father had little to say about the indefinite interruption to her budding career.

Possibly because he could see absolutely no other solution to the present emergency. If Anna were not to take over the running of the household and the eventual care of her mother, who could? He accepted things as they had to be.

So did Anna. And, to her credit, with singularly little rebellion, even in her own heart and mind. The one person who did express profound indignation on her behalf was, surprisingly enough, Roderick Delawney.

True to his promise, he had made enquiries about her mother's progress the very next day and, after that, at intervals of a few days. He was, he told Anna, when he met her one morning in the High Street, at home for a few weeks on holiday, and he asked her, quite as though he had a right to know, how she was herself managing to have indefinite leave from wherever she worked.

"I'm not employed anywhere. I'm still only just emerging from the student stage," Anna said, and then she found herself explaining at some length about her musical aspirations.

"But surely this is just the wrong moment to break off and be missing from the scene?" he exclaimed with genuine concern. "If you're beginning to get small engagements and good crits you need to keep on registering an appearance. Can't you get a housekeeper or someone to look after your father, and then a nurse when your mother comes home?"

Suppressing an impulse to ask him how much he thought all that would cost, Anna smilingly shook her head.

"I don't like the interruption, of course," she conceded. "And, as you say, it couldn't have come at a more unfortunate time. But no one can have everything as they want it, and Mother must come first. The only thing I – " she stopped, remembering with a stab of quite agonising regret how she had floated on a cloud of glory for just a

44

few golden moments after she realised that both Jonathan Keyne and the great Warrender himself had found her impressively worthwhile as an artist.

"Yes?" he prompted. "What is the only thing you just can't reconcile yourself to?"

"How do you know that was what I was going to say?" But her faint smile told him he had guessed correctly. "Well, you see, on the very afternoon of the operation I was auditioned for something very special. I know he – they were genuinely impressed. But I just had to turn it down then and there."

"But look here – !"

"No, please! And don't tell a soul. I don't know quite why I told you, except that you're so very kind and sympathetic. But my father has no idea and would be in despair if he knew. He has quite enough to worry him already without indulging in vain regrets on my behalf."

"You really are a good kid! A bit too good for your own advantage, I'm inclined to think." And he frowned with the air of a man who was used to bulldozing his way to what *he* wanted even if other people's interests stood in the way. "I wish I could do something. Suppose I ask Teresa – my sister – to find something for you in this festival of hers? Would that help?"

"It's terribly kind of you." For a moment Anna's hand lingered gratefully on his arm. "But at the moment I simply can't make any plans except to look after my mother when she comes out of hospital."

"Well – " he shrugged as though accepting her decision for the moment, but for the moment only. And Anna went on her way home, sufficiently comforted by his concern to find the courage to write three difficult but necessary letters.

The first was to Madame Marburger, explaining that

her mother's serious illness necessitated her giving up her lessons for an indefinite period. The second was to Carrie, asking her to send on the rest of her things and to make arrangements to find another girl to share the flat as it was impossible to say how long it would be before Anna could return to London. And the third one was to Judy, giving a brief outline of her present dilemma and asking if she could find out Jonathan Keyne's address from the London telephone directory.

"I feel I should write a few lines to him," she wrote carefully to Judy, "as I owe him some sort of apology for just dropping out of the scene after he had shown genuine interest."

Madame Marburger's regrets, expressed formally but with some feeling, came by return of post. "I fully understand that you cannot desert your parents at this point," she wrote. "But keep in practice, and remember that you were so near to success that it would be almost a sin to give up now. I am not in the habit of over-praising my students, but I think I should tell you that you are among the few I have had through my hands who *possibly* possess the divine spark."

Anna was cheered at first to receive this praise. But then she found herself suddenly weeping a few reluctant tears for the present quenching of her divine spark.

Carrie, for her part, made prompt and efficient arrangements to send on Anna's possessions, and added a note to say there was no need to worry about the re-letting of her share of the flat. An Australian cousin had turned up and was only too glad to take on the accommodation.

Judy's letter was naturally longer and more personal than either of the others, and was full of indignant sympathy for the ill luck which had befallen her friend.

"I searched the phone directory for Keyne's address,"

she wrote, "but he seems to be ex-directory. And when I made some enquiries around the office I was told that he left London a few days ago and probably won't be back for any length of time until he starts rehearsals for the Canadian tour. I should think *he* will get in touch with *you* if he really wants you, and the letter will no doubt be sent on to you. Maddening to have to wait again, my poor pet, I know. But that seems to be all you can do."

Anna, who had not told Judy anything of the final audition, folded up the letter with a sigh. Even now she winced at the thought of what she had missed – and much, much more of the way in which she had missed it. Her whole behaviour during those last few moments with Jonathan Keyne now seemed to her so deplorably silly and irresponsible that she simply had not had the courage to tell Judy. And what he himself must have thought she really could not imagine.

If she had been able to write him a short letter of apology and explanation it would not have been so bad. But now it seemed that she must remain in his memory – if she remained there at all – as a stupid, ill-behaved, entirely unreliable exhibitionist.

It would have been a melancholy day indeed for her if she had not gone to the hospital that afternoon and found that her mother had at last taken a real step on the road to recovery. For the first time she looked something like her real self – except, of course, that it was difficult to imagine Mother lying languidly in bed in ordinary circumstances. But she smiled her humorous little smile and asked in a rather low voice how Anna and her father were coping.

Until that moment she had seemed completely indifferent to the way anyone was coping, so long as she need not make any effort herself – a state of things so alien to Anna's lifelong experience that this alone would have convinced her that her mother was dangerously ill. But now she was smiling faintly and looked really interested.

"It's simplicity itself," Anna assured her enthusiastically. "I don't expect I look after things half as well as you do. But Dad seems quite satisfied and, to tell the truth, I'm rather enjoying a bit of cooking and housework. I suppose it's a novelty."

"But your own work, dear?" A small worried frown creased her mother's forehead, prompting Anna to the most determined invention – anything so that the dangerous shadow of worry should be banished.

"Well, it's the most extraordinary thing, Mother. Just a day or two before you were taken ill, I was auditioned for a short opera tour some time next year, and I was taken on. It isn't until quite a way on in the year and I have to prepare several roles. That means I can work at home, part of the time with Dad. It couldn't be better, could it?"

"Anna dear, how wonderful!" Her mother smiled almost brilliantly. "And you're sure you can work satisfactorily at home?"

"It's the very thing I would have chosen to do," declared Anna, a good deal astonished herself to find how adroitly she had mingled fact and fiction. "So, you see, there's absolutely nothing for you to worry about."

"I'm so glad. Now I don't mind so much about going away and leaving your father."

"L-leaving him?" stammered Anna, chill with terror. But her mother laughed. Faintly but, characteristically enough, with real humour.

"Oh, don't worry. I'm not going to die," she said firmly. "I'm *really* not going to die, after all, Anna. But the doctor was talking to me this morning, and he wants me to go away to a convalescent home for at least a month, between leaving here and going home."

"Why, of course, dear, if that's the best thing for you!"

"Much the best thing, now that I know you'll be looking after Dad," said her mother. Then she closed her eyes contentedly and was almost instantly asleep.

Realising that she had stayed the full length of the permitted visit, Anna stole from the room and went out into the late autumn sunshine. She was infinitely relieved by her mother's undoubted improvement, and only faintly guilty at the thought of the lies she had so glibly told. What did fret her was the knowledge that a largely idle month or six weeks now stretched in front of her. Her domestic duties were light indeed, for her father was the least demanding of men and the small house an easy one to run. There was little she could do except a student's routine practice, whereas, if things had been different, these were almost certainly the weeks in which she would have been working hard to perfect her roles for Jonathan Keyne's Canadian tour.

"It's no good even thinking about it," she told herself almost savagely. And at that moment she became aware that someone was sounding a musical motor-horn with some insistence.

Anna glanced up and saw that a small, elegant white car was parked at the kerb, while the driver – a girl in a brilliant scarlet jacket – was waving somewhat imperiously. Realising that she herself was the only person within reasonable distance, Anna went forward, expecting to be asked for directions to some place or other.

Instead, the girl – who, in her dark, flashing beauty, seemed as brilliant as the jacket she was wearing – said, "You are Anna Fulroyd, aren't you?"

"Yes, I am." Anna looked enquiring.

"I'm Teresa Delawney. My brother was telling me about you." The girl gave Anna a perfectly beautiful smile which almost – though not quite – disguised the ruthless determination in her vivid face. "He says you have a tremendous amount of know-how about the musical world. Is that right?"

"I don't think I could make such an extravagant claim for myself." Anna smiled irresistibly because the other girl was so pretty and so intent on what she wanted. "I'm a singing student at what I suppose one could call a rather advanced stage, but – "

"Oh, I wasn't interested in your musical *studies*," Teresa Delawney explained with devastating candour. "But you know about the musical world as such, don't you? terms and personalities and how to deal with temperamental people and that sort of thing?" Then, before Anna could even draw breath to answer that, she added, "And do you type?"

"As a matter of fact, I do," admitted Anna, wondering what this had to do with what the girl called "musical know-how". "I'm not an expert typist, but – "

"You'd be good enough for what I want. Jump in." The other girl opened the car door, evidently expecting Anna to drop her own unimportant concerns on the instant. "I'm going to take you home with me and we'll have a good talk."

And so positive was she about the priority of her own wishes over everything else that Anna, to her subsequent astonishment, found herself actually obeying Teresa Delawney to the letter.

The speed and skill with which she was then conveyed to Coppershaw Grange left Anna rather breathless. Teresa Delawney took no stupid risks, but she drove with a confidence in her own right of way that was very nearly regal.

Coppershaw Grange, which stood about a mile and a

half outside the town, was a Regency house of quite superb design and construction. Big enough to be imposing, but elegant enough to be almost endearing. And it stood in several acres of very lovely parkland.

Anna had never been as near as the porticoed entrance before, and when she had stepped out of the car, she stood there for a minute, just enjoying the lovely sight of the house.

"What a beautiful place to live," she exclaimed quite frankly, and the other girl cast a glance along the wide façade, a little as though she were seeing her home for the first time.

"Yes, it is rather nice, isn't it?" she agreed. "And it's ideally suited for what I want." All too obviously, even her lovely home was little more than a background for her own wishes, and without further comment she led Anna up the short flight of steps and into the big panelled entrance hall.

Here she hardly gave Anna time even to glance round before she almost hustled her through the house into the most beautiful drawing-room Anna had ever seen. All along one side long windows reached to the floor, giving a magnificent view across an ornamental terrace to sloping gardens beyond.

"This is where we shall have the two concerts of chamber music, of course," Teresa Delawney explained rapidly. "It's a pity we're coming into the chilly part of the year, otherwise we could have used the terrace and gardens."

"Why didn't you make it a summer festival?" Anna asked. "This lovely place is just made for it."

"Oh, I didn't want to wait until *next year*!" Teresa Delawney's tone suggested that she was measuring out aeons of time. "I like to do things when I *want* to do them.

If you wait, ideas go stale on you, and then you don't want the thing when you've got it."

Anna found this a rather revealing statement, but she merely observed mildly that even the most modest festival required a good deal of preparation.

"It's not like throwing an impromptu party," she added with a laugh.

"But with me things have to be like an impromptu party," Teresa countered firmly. "That's the whole fun of the thing. What's the good of having a father who's disgustingly rich and very indulgent if you can't make large, extravagant gestures? I always think it must have been wonderful to be one of those French kings at Versailles who could order a ball or a masque or even an opera, and all the artists of the period just ran around and poured out their gifts to make it a real success. I wish I'd lived then."

"There must have been disadvantages for some people in that arrangement," Anna said, still smiling. "Anyway, I'm afraid it's very different today, when people make their plans a long while ahead and – "

"You needn't tell me about the difficulties. I know them, and I refuse to recognise them," Teresa interrupted. "Anyway, don't be defeatist. You're going to have to be a lot more positive than this if you're going to help me organise this festival."

"Help you organise – ? But I haven't said I'll do any such thing. I'm not even qual – "

"Of course you have. Why did you get into the car otherwise? Anyway, sit down and I'll tell you what has been arranged so far."

And while Anna – annoyed but intrigued against her will – sank into a chair without further protest, Teresa Delawney went over to a beautiful inlaid writing desk from which she produced two large files. She brought these back, spread them out on a table in front of her and proceeded to outline her plans with quite amazing clarity and precision.

If she had not, in the process, displayed a touch of something which almost amounted to genius, Anna would have found some way of backing out of the arrangement. But within minutes she was interested and fascinated to a degree she would never have believed possible. For, with a mixture of ruthless determination and undoubted vision, Teresa Delawney had already laid the foundations of a minor festival of genuine interest and novelty.

"You ought to have been an impresario," declared Anna at one point, and although she laughed as she said it, she more than half meant it.

"I think so too," agreed the other girl, who was evidently unhampered by anything like false modesty. "Of course it helps a lot having my father's money behind me. But I reckon we can put on a couple of weeks of festival that the people around here won't forget in a hurry. The house itself will provide the background for the chamber music, the piano recital by Franz Klein, and the final Eighteenth Century Evening which will be primarily a private party – in fancy dress, of course – but will include dances of the period by eight dancers from the Athena Ballet Company –"

"How on earth did you get *them*?" Anna interrupted.

"Oh, the right price and the pulling of a string or two," replied Teresa airily. "The Tithe Barn has been transformed into a small countrified theatre, and the very good amateur company from Elthorne, laced with a few professionals, are giving three performances of 'Past and Present' –"

"The review by Bannister and Tom Mallender, you mean?"

"Yes. And I've even got Gail Bannister, who made

such a success in it, to do the famous Spanish number."

"I can't believe it!" Anna spoke with genuine admiration. "How on earth did you *do* all this?"

"I had one or two massive strokes of luck," Teresa conceded, though she evidently greatly enjoyed Anna's uninhibited praise. "The biggest piece of luck was having the co-operation of Jonathan Keyne, I suppose."

"J-Jonathan Keyne?" A prickle of shock – both terrifying and delightful – ran all the way down Anna's spine. "Do you know him, then?"

"Very well. Do you?"

"Only slightly." With an effort Anna recaptured her self-control. "What – what else had you in mind? Or is this the full programme?"

"Certainly not! I want a concert of some sort in the Tithe Barn and I'd like something in the church, if you think your father could put on something really up to the standard of the rest."

"I don't see why he shouldn't," Anna said rather coldly, for she greatly resented this slighting reference to her father who, after all, was far more of a genuine musician and a professional than this attitudinising young woman would ever be.

"Well, I meant – not just another dreary oratorio performance that everyone has heard a dozen times before, you know. And of course only the *pick* of the choir. There's one kid there who is quite outstanding, I'm told."

"Tommy Bream," said Anna, choking back her chagrin sufficiently at least to name the blessing and bane of most choir practices.

"Yes, I think that was the name. Talk to your father about it, will you? But of course we've got to work to a very high standard."

"Of course." Anna's tone was still warningly cool,

but the other girl seemed unaware of that. "And where in all this did you want me to operate?"

"I told you! You'll be at the organising end, here with me in the house. There's a tremendous amount of secretarial work to be done, people to interview, hand-outs to local papers and possibly even some of the national ones. You might have some ideas about the concert in the Tithe Barn too. And then there'll be advance ticket selling to attend to. Oh, there's no end to the ways in which I can use you."

Anna was not a conceited girl and had never had an exaggerated idea of her own attainments. But the expression "the ways in which I can use you" was not a flattering one, while the calm assumption that naturally her role could be only that of general dogsbody was so enraging that for a moment she could not even find the voice to utter her contemptuous refusal of the offered appointment.

And then, into the short silence which succeeded Teresa's careless assessment of Anna and the ways in which she could make herself useful, there intruded the sounds of someone arriving in the hall outside.

Immediately Teresa sprang to her feet and, completely ignoring Anna or anything she had been going to say, she ran to the door with an exclamation of surprise and delight.

As she did so, the door opened and Jonathan Keyne walked into the room.

CHAPTER THREE

"Why, Jonathan!" To Anna's somewhat irrational resentment, Teresa reached up and kissed the man who had just come in. "I didn't expect you until this evening."

"I got away sooner than I dared to hope." He lightly returned the kiss before, looking past her, he saw Anna and exclaimed in a cool, not very friendly tone, "Hello! What brings you here?"

Teresa switched round, an angry light in her eyes, and replied for Anna before she could even open her lips.

"Miss Fulroyd is helping me with some festival details. Her father is the local organist here – " the tone somehow reduced him to a very minor status – "so it seemed a good idea to enlist her help."

"As one of the artists for your festival?"

"Oh, no!" Teresa dismissed that quaint notion with a laugh. "She's just doing some of the office jobs for me."

"I see." If there was a touch of irony in his tone she did not seem to notice it. And in any case, the conversation was turned into fresh channels by the arrival at that moment of Roderick Delawney.

His greeting to Jonathan Keyne was casual but friendly. Then he, in his turn, took in Anna's presence and exclaimed, "Aha! So you've joined the festival bandwagon, after all?"

"Not exactly," Anna began. But once more Teresa insisted on answering for her.

"Miss Fulroyd has promised to take on some of the organising chores for me," she said quickly. "She's going to be such a help! We've just had a long talk and she's starting right in tomorrow morning. At least, I hope she is." And Teresa flung Anna her brilliant, compelling smile.

This was, of course, the moment to tell Teresa Delawney – crisply if not vulgarly – exactly what she could do with her organising plans for the Festival. Anna even drew breath to do so. But then, in a way she could neither avoid nor define, Jonathan Keyne caught her glance and held it, a sort of interested speculation in his eyes.

And because – ever since that first encounter some years ago now – she had wanted passionately to secure Jonathan Keyne's interest, she simply could not make herself say the words that would banish her finally and irrevocably from the festival scene.

Instead, she heard herself say, formally but pleasantly, "I'll start tomorrow if that suits you. But I must go now. My father will be wondering where I am."

"I'll drive you home," stated Jonathan Keyne unexpectedly.

"No, you won't!" Oddly enough, brother and sister spoke in unison, though with totally different expressions.

"You're not running off the moment you've arrived." Teresa caught Keyne's arm with a smiling little air which was almost, but not quite, proprietorial. "You must be more than ready for tea after your long journey."

And Roderick said, "I'll drive you down, Anna. The car's just outside."

There was nothing to do then but accept Roderick Delawney's offer with the best grace possible, make her good-byes and leave. Teresa gave her a smiling but definitely dismissing little nod and said,

"Nine-thirty tomorrow. I'm an early starter, and I have

to go out later in the morning."

Jonathan Keyne said nothing at all, merely inclined his head with that speculative glance again, and then turned away to talk to Teresa.

Roderick took Anna's arm lightly and ushered her through the house once more and out to the waiting car. As he did so he said, slightly lowering his voice, "I made sure you were going to join the list of artists when I found you there with Teresa and Keyne. How come you're contenting yourself with an office job?"

"Perhaps I'm not festival standard." She managed to smile quite good-humouredly over that.

"Aren't you really?" he asked, with pleasing directness.

"I don't know." She laughed, but she bit her lip too, for her artistic pride had taken some battering during the last hour or so. "It's not for me to say. But, in any case, with the responsibility of my mother in the background, I don't think I should take on any professional commitment in the next few months."

"Not even something actually on the spot? That seems nonsense to me. How much will your mother need your undivided attention in the immediate future?"

"For the next four or six weeks not at all," Anna confessed. "I heard this afternoon that she is to go to a convalescent home for some while after leaving hospital, but – "

"Well, there you are! You could well involve yourself in this Festival, and at the same time be available when your mother needs you. Why not?"

"For one thing, Mr. Delawney, I haven't been asked." She smiled a little wryly.

"Don't call me Mr. Delawney. It sounds ridiculous now we're more or less family friends. Call me Rod. Most of my friends do."

"Very well, then – Rod." She turned her head and smiled at him with genuine warmth, for his friendliness was welcome after Jonathan Keyne's coolness and Teresa's mixture of patronage and command. "It's very kind of you to be exercised on my behalf. But even with a family festival, as you might say, casting isn't done on a purely friendly basis, I feel sure. You don't know anything about my artistic standing, and anyway, your sister has very definite views on what she wants. Her ideas are good ones, too. I could tell that, even from a preliminary discussion. I don't think she would welcome any friendly interference, even by you."

He laughed reluctantly.

"Teresa doesn't welcome any sort of interference with her plans on any basis," he observed, though without rancour. "And she rates me as no more than a cheerful Philistine – which I am, up to a point, of course. But I tell you one thing – I'd like Jonathan to hear you. He really does know."

"He *has* heard me," said Anna before she could stop herself.

"He has?" Roderick Delawney looked interested. "And what did he think of you? Do you know?"

"Rather well – I believe."

"Then why not – ?"

"No, no, let it ride," she said urgently. "Whatever he thought of me, I had occasion to annoy him professionally, I'm afraid. It wouldn't be good tactics to – push myself at this point. I'd rather be overlooked than noticed by him at the moment."

"You're a funny girl," he declared as he stopped the car before the small white house where Anna and her father lived. "I never knew anyone so diffident about pressing her claims. In my limited experience professional performers just can't wait to let you know how good they are."

"Perhaps," Anna said with a smile, as she got out of the car, "it's because I'm not exactly a professional yet. But thank you, Rod. Your appreciation has done me a lot of good. Only don't talk to Jonathan Keyne about me, will you?"

"Not if you say not." He laughed a little vexedly before he waved to her and drove off, leaving her to enter the house in a state of mind curiously balanced between excitement and dejection.

Her father immediately came out into the passage to enquire anxiously about her long absence, having evidently begun to link this in his mind with possible bad news from the hospital. But Anna hastened to re-assure him and then explained that she had spent most of the afternoon at Coppershaw Grange, discussing the local Festival with Teresa Delawney.

"Really?" Her father looked relieved, but again seemed inclined to brush off the Delawneys' excursion into the arts as little more than childish posturing. "Was there anything serious to discuss?"

"Well, yes, I'm bound to say there was." Anna smiled, but there was a note of respect in her voice. "You won't believe it, but Teresa Delawney has some quite astounding ideas, and a very capable – not to say ruthless – way of pursuing what she wants. Frankly, Dad, if I'm any judge, she's going to make a success of this thing." And she proceeded to give some details of Teresa's plans.

"Well, unlimited money can do a great deal, of course," her father admitted good-humouredly. "Particularly if it's allied to a certain degree of judgment. Jonathan Keyne should supply some real professionalism. What part is he playing exactly?"

"I'm not quite sure. She said she had been tremendously lucky to have his friendly co-operation. I suppose he'll act in an advisory capacity of some sort. And then obviously he would be able to pull strings when it came to engaging some eminent artists."

"Is there any suggestion that you should sing?" her father asked.

"None at all." Anna's tone was crisp and decided. "I'm simply on the organising side."

"What made you take that on?" her father looked curious.

"I liked the idea of being in it somewhere, I suppose," she said with a smiling little shrug. But she added nothing about Teresa's faintly patronising attitude and nothing about the way Jonathan Keyne's thoughtful glance had made her feel that she must be in this Festival somewhere, somehow.

Instead, she went on to explain that Teresa seemed to think there should be something included in connection with the church and choir. And here again she suppressed any reference to Teresa's slighting remarks in this direction.

"A concert of church music, you mean?" her father looked considering. "Well, the setting would be exceptionally beautiful, of course, and the choir is unusually good this year. As for solo singing, Tommy Bream may be a limb of Satan, but he is the best boy soprano for miles around. Given the right choice of anthem, he can give the impression of being one of God's chosen angels. Local people are used to him, of course. But if Miss Delawney is expecting people from other parts of the country –"

"We want something really unusual as the centre point," Anna interrupted eagerly. "Dad, haven't you

61

something among your many compositions that could be included? I know your heart's in opera, but you have done other things, haven't you? Wouldn't it be wonderful if we had a local *composition* as well as local performers?"

"No, no –" Her father shook his head with unexpected emphasis. "No question of it."

"Don't turn it down without considering it!" Anna exclaimed.

"But I'm afraid I must, my dear. You see, I've come to the conclusion lately that I have been deluding myself all these years –"

"Dad, what nonsense!"

"No." He spoke without bitterness but with finality. "You come to a time, Anna, when – however optimistic you may be – you have to accept the verdict of practical experience. I've done a lot of thinking lately. Particularly since your mother has been away and so ill. And it's gradually come to me that I'm probably not a composer at all. I'm just a church organist who loves music and can play rather effectively with notes."

"That simply isn't true," cried Anna indignantly. "You may have thought on too vast and grandiose a scale." The truth came rushing out without any tactful attempt at checking it. "But you are a true music-maker, I know you are. The ideas are there, but not the practical form. That lovely thing you were playing that evening after choir practice –"

"This, you mean?" Her father went to the piano and began to sketch in the melody which had so entranced Anna before.

"Yes! That's it! Then you did remember what I meant?"

"I recalled it after you'd gone." Her father ran his

hands lovingly over the keys. "It modulates into the minor key here – or I think that's how it should go."

"Of course it should." She sang a few phrases along with the piano accompaniment. "It's much too good to lose. Couldn't you use it in some way? Surely you could?"

"Well, as a matter of fact," he said unexpectedly, "I have."

"You *have*?"

Her father nodded and suddenly he looked almost bashful, like a boy instead of a tired, elderly man who had suffered more anxiety than he could well bear during recent weeks.

"I began to develop the theme after you mentioned it. And it seems to me that, as the central melody of a song cycle –"

"What song cycle?" Anna's question was sharp enough almost to make him wince. But she was suddenly desperately afraid that, even now, the elusive loveliness of his musical thought might be smothered beneath an over-weighted form of words.

"Well – " her father went over to his desk, rummaged about and presently came back with a few typewritten sheets of paper at which Anna gazed in growing alarm. "I suppose – " he was still smiling that slight, shy smile – "it's astonishing and even embarrassing for young people to find that their parents ever wrote poetry. But years ago I used to indulge myself that way."

He held out the sheets of paper to her and she took them with a reluctance she could hardly conceal. How awful! He wrote *poetry* in addition to those turgid opera libretti. And now she was going to have to argue for the life of that lovely air against the weight of uninspired words.

As she resentfully scanned the first few lines they

seemed to run together, conveying nothing to her resistant mind. And then something clicked in her mind and she gave a sort of gasp of relief.

The verses were charming! She had to admit that. Not great poetry, of course, but singularly lilting in an unpretentious way. Eminently singable, for one thing. As a singer herself, she sensed that immediately. And, as she read on, she felt almost certain that, set to the right music, these conventional but rather beautiful verses could have an extraordinary appeal.

There were four poems dealing, predictably enough, with reactions to the four seasons. But though there was a pastoral tranquillity about some of them, in others there was an unexpected touch of human passion. Hardly able to associate all this with her father – for, after all, which of us associates passion, or even pastoral tranquillity, with a familiar parent? – Anna read on until the end.

Then she put down the sheets and said with conviction, "You know, it's good! and it's singable. Do you mean that you've been setting all this to music in the last few weeks?"

"I did some work on it earlier," her father admitted. "But somehow, when I was so worried and unhappy about your mother, it was a way of expressing my hopes and fears – and my fondness for her. It sounds silly in an elderly man, I daresay – "

"It does nothing of the sort!" stated Anna, hugging him. "It sounds lovely and touching and worthwhile. And Mother will be overjoyed about it."

"Well, well – " her father kissed her and laughed in a deprecating way – "it should make at least an acceptable song cycle for organ, choir and soprano. And some of those higher passages lie beautifully for young Tommy,

64

if I can drill them into him."

"It's going to be wonderful," Anna declared. "Finish it as soon as you can. And we'll make it the sensation of the Festival!"

"I don't know about that."

But she realised that, for the first time since her mother had been rushed to hospital, her father was looking eager and lively again.

No one had made any suggestions about how she should reach Coppershaw Grange by nine-thirty the following morning. But Anna knew that a somewhat infrequent bus passed within ten minutes' walk of the Grange and, having checked the timetable at the bus stop near her home, she saw to it that she and her father breakfasted quite early. Then she set off to her first morning's work with mixed feelings, but a general sense of starting on something exciting.

She had walked only a few yards up the road, however, when she realised that an open car was parked near the kerb and, as she came towards it, Jonathan Keyne got out of the driving seat and came round to open the near-side door.

"Why, what brings you here at this hour?" she exclaimed.

"You do," he informed her. "Get in and I'll drive you up to the Grange."

"But surely you didn't come on purpose to fetch me?" She was impressed, even faintly embarrassed, by the thought.

"Not entirely," he assured her. "It is, as you see, a wonderful morning. I wanted to get something of the feel of the place. Also to have a look at the church, in case we include a church concert. At the same time, I hadn't heard of any plans to get you to the Grange in time for what Teresa calls an early start. How were you proposing to come, by the way?"

"By bus, of course. One passes fairly near the gates of the Grange."

"Quarter of an hour's walk away, so the butler assured me."

"Perhaps," Anna said demurely, "I walk a little faster than the butler. In any case, a walk on such a morning isn't going to harm anyone."

"Agreed. But I hope you find the lift a good idea instead."

"I do. And thank you very much. But now I am going to be rather too early."

"No, you aren't," he assured her. "We're going to drive around the lanes a little, and you're going to explain the ridiculous way you behaved to me when we last met in London. You'll need to make it good too. I don't easily forgive people who make a fool of me."

"I didn't make a fool of you!" she exclaimed distressfully.

"Of course you did. How much eloquence do you suppose I had had to spill on a knowledgeable old bird like Warrender in order to convince him that it was worth risking an absolute beginner as one of the central props of my company?"

"Were you – were you thinking of me as one of the central props of your company?" she asked, awed.

"I was," he said grimly. "I didn't know then that you were totally unreliable, of course."

"I'm *not* totally unreliable!"

"What else? You let me stake my personal judgment on you, right up to the point of my offering you a contract. And then you threw a ridiculous emotional scene of refusal and rushed away, leaving me to tell Warrender that I'd backed someone who didn't want the chance after all, thanks. You even told me to 'leave you alone' – " he reproduced her exact tone of distracted protest with some cruelty – "as though I'd made some improper proposal to you. If that's not making a fool of someone, what is?"

"You don't understand." She was trembling, but she managed to keep her voice steady. "I'd just had an upsetting phone call and – "

He pulled the car to the side of the lane and stopped it with such a jerk that her sentence was bitten off in the middle.

"She'd had an upsetting phone call!" he said to the countryside in general. Then he raised his hands and dropped them back on the steering wheel. "You were being offered the kind of chance any young artist might ask God on her knees for – and an upsetting phone call put you off your stroke. What was upsetting about it, for heaven's sake?" His tone was almost savage. "Had your unimportant boy-friend stood you up for another girl or something?"

"No," Anna said coldly and distinctly. "My mother was thought to be dying."

"Oh – " he did look taken aback at that. "I'm sorry."

"Don't mention it," she retorted icily.

And after a moment he said, rather sulkily, "Did she – die?"

"No. She recovered, after all, I'm thankful to say. She is very slowly recovering completely, we're daring to hope. But that's why I'm down here now, looking after my father and expecting to look after my mother when she comes from convalescent home in some weeks' time."

"And meanwhile – " his tone sounded reasonable but

somehow slightly dangerous – "what happens to your career?"

"It must wait, I'm afraid."

He started the car again after that. And after a few minutes he said, "I feel bound to tell you, my dear, that is not the way careers are built. If you allow yourself to be put off by every family crisis – " He stopped, evidently sensing he was going a little too far.

"Do go on," said Anna sweetly.

"Look, I don't want to sound callous. But if you're going to make a name for yourself in what's possibly the most competitive profession in the world, you're going to have to get your priorities right from the very beginning. I'm sure you were badly scared, but – your mother did recover, didn't she?"

"She might not have."

"But she did," he insisted obstinately. "And because you panicked unnecessarily you missed the chance of a lifetime. These chances don't tend to come again," he added deliberately.

"I take your point," she said coldly. Then she glanced pointedly at her watch and added, "Isn't it time we made for the Grange? It's twenty past nine."

He reversed the car and, with a rather heavy silence between them, they made for Coppershaw Grange. Only when they were in sight of the entrance did he speak again, and his tone was almost reflective as he said,

"Anthea Warrender – she was Anthea Benton then – once faced a decision very similar to yours. *Her* mother was ill and she wanted to drop everything and rush home. But Warrender had just arranged for her to appear, as a substitute for someone else, at Covent Garden for the first time. He insisted on her staying – and that was the start of her great career."

"The point of this cautionary tale being, I suppose, that the masterful male must always be listened to," said Anna drily. "What did Warrender do – pat her on the head?"

"No. He married her," replied Jonathan Keyne with a grin, as he stopped the car in front of the house.

"Would you call that reward or punishment?" said Anna rather pertly. "Thanks for the lift." And she got out of the car and ran up the steps to the house, while he looked after her with a slightly intrigued expression.

Teresa Delawney was waiting for her in a pleasant room which was obviously half office, half sitting room. It looked out on the front drive, which meant she had probably seen Anna arrive in Jonathan Keyne's car. But she made no reference to this. She was very businesslike this morning, with quite a stack of routine correspondence ready for Anna's attention. And she made it clear that she expected the same standard of efficiency from others that she herself displayed.

Anna, who made no pretensions to being a secretary, was hard put to it in the first hour and a half to live up to these expectations. After that, however, she began to get the hang of what was required of her and, since she was genuinely interested in almost every aspect of the work, she found herself enjoying it. There was little sign of the previous friendly way of involving her in discussion, but Anna accepted the fact that work must come first, and it was not until they were relaxing over excellent mid-morning coffee that she said,

"I spoke to my father about a concert in the church, and he seems to think that something quite interesting could be arranged."

"Oh, well – we'll have to see." For the first time, Teresa sounded almost vague. "It's so difficult to get anything unusual within that framework. What sort of novelty, for instance, can one have in a church concert?"

Anna bit her lip, suppressed her irritation and said quietly, "My father is something of a composer, and he has done a lovely song cycle which – "

"He's not a composer of any eminence, though, is he?" cut in Teresa disparagingly.

"No, I couldn't claim that," Anna admitted. "But this particular work – "

"Well, as I say, we should have to see." Teresa's tone practically sank the song cycle without trace. "It's no good putting something forward just because it happens to have been manufactured locally, as you might say." She could have been speaking of a new-fangled dustbin. "Local pride has been the kiss of death to more than one musical or theatrical enterprise, hasn't it?"

Anna could find no civil answer to this, so she remained silent. But she wondered now, with passionate resentment, why she had ever allowed herself to be involved in this undertaking. And, because she did not want to face an unwelcome truth, she refused to admit that the one answer was – Jonathan Keyne.

"I shall be out all the afternoon," Teresa informed her presently. "But you might start compiling those lists of people who will need details of performances and tickets, and later – in certain cases – invitations to the private affairs. I'll have lunch sent in for you on a tray, and if I don't get back before you leave, can you be here to-morrow again about the same time?"

Anna said briefly that she could. But she added firmly, "Tomorrow afternoon, however, I shall want to go to the hospital. My mother won't be there much longer, and I want to see something of her before she goes to the convalescent home."

"Yes, of course." Teresa was quite good-humoured about that. "And perhaps you would like some flowers and fruit for her from the greenhouses?"

The offer was casual, but obviously well meant and, while Anna accepted with becoming gratitude, she tried hard to think a little more kindly of the spoiled girl who dispensed insults and favours with such remarkable impartiality.

Presently Teresa left her and after a few minutes Anna saw her drive off in the smart little white car. After that her lunch – a good one – was brought to her on a tray, and while she ate it with unfeigned enjoyment she reflected, without rancour, that she was evidently not to be regarded as a member of any house party. If she had been one of the Festival artists it would, of course, have been different. But she was not an artist. She had forfeited her claim to anything of that sort. She was just secretary and general dogsbody to Teresa Delawney.

With minor variations, this was the pattern of Anna's life during the next few days. Most mornings she caught the bus, and it was perfectly true that there was no hardship in the very beautiful ten minutes' walk from the bus stop to the Grange. Once, when the weather broke, Rod Delawney fetched her by car, and once Teresa herself picked her up when she happened to be in town on some other errand.

Of Jonathan Keyne Anna saw very little beyond an occasional glimpse of him in the house. Certainly he made no further attempt to drive her either to or from her work.

Every other afternoon she went to the hospital to see her mother, who was now well enough to be greatly entertained by Anna's lively account of the projected Festival.

71

"But you ought to have some real place in it yourself," objected Mrs. Fulroyd. "Something other than just doing office jobs for Teresa Delawney, I mean. You are probably much the most gifted singer in the district. You'd think the Delawneys would be only too glad to include you."

"I don't think I have any place in Teresa's plans." With some effort Anna kept her tone light and a little amused. "And Rod – her brother – doesn't have any say in her arrangements."

"What about the parents? It's her father, isn't it, who supplies all the money? And what about Mrs. Delawney? I've always heard that she's very much to the fore in anything to do with her family."

"I haven't met either of them yet," Anna explained. "I think they're away visiting friends or relations. But they're due back in a day or two."

In actual fact, the older Delawneys returned home the following day and Anna met them for the first time.

Mr. Delawney confined himself to a nod and a couple of words when they were introduced, very casually, by Teresa. He was a silent, self-made man, justly proud of the fact that he owed his quite staggering wealth to his own good brain, but disinclined to discuss that or anything else with any but a few chosen cronies. He had few interests outside his business empire, but one of these was his daughter, of whom he was inordinately proud. And, after watching them together for no more than a few minutes, Anna thought she saw one good reason, at any rate, why Teresa found it difficult to imagine a world where her wishes were not of primary importance.

Mrs. Delawney was an entirely different proposition from her husband. She had, in the common phrase, married beneath her. That was to say, she came of good but impoverished stock and, although she had not hesitated to marry money when the opportunity arose, she reserved to herself the right to appear to be above anything so vulgar as the mere making of money. This did not mean that she had any inhibitions about spending it. Not ostentatiously, but with a genuine degree of taste and cultural judgment. She entirely approved of her daughter's plans for a local Festival. Not because, like her husband, she wished to indulge Teresa – on the contrary, she was much more clear-sighted and critical about their daughter than he was – but because she judged this to be a completely admirable and tasteful way of spending a great deal of money.

With something between awe and amusement Anna saw how completely Teresa combined her father's drive and efficiency with her mother's taste and artistic judgment. It was a formidable combination, and she could not help wondering how attractive that combination might be to Jonathan Keyne.

Unlike the men of the family, Mrs. Delawny put forward *her* views on the Festival with trenchant candour, quite irrespective of whether or not they coincided with her daughter's wishes. It was she who, unexpectedly, came down firmly on the side of including a church concert in the programme.

"Of course we must!" she said, ignoring the fact that her daughter resented the "we". "The church is the most beautiful in this part of England, and the choir is of a very high standard indeed. I know because I sometimes go to church, though you may not, Teresa. As for that boy soprano – Tommy Somebody – he is quite outstanding. And your father, Miss Fulroyd, is a credit to us all," she added graciously. "He even composes, I believe?"

"Yes, he does." Anna gave her a quick, shy smile, and

was about to enlarge on the subject of the song cycle when Teresa said,

"Oh, Mother, so do most church organists. Bits and pieces to keep the audience – I mean the congregation – happy until the bride arrives, and that sort of thing."

"Mr. Fulroyd composes operas, I understand," replied Mrs. Delawney firmly.

"None of which have been performed," retorted her daughter crisply. And then, as though even she realised that any discussion on these lines must prove embarrassing to all, she added quite sweetly, "Oh, Anna – " they had reached Christian names terms by now – "I wonder if you could find me that letter from Franz Klein. I'm nearly sure I left it on the piano in the big drawing-room."

Anna knew she had not. But she too realised this was an excuse to get rid of her while an embarrassing argument took place. So she rose immediately and went to the big drawing-room, where she managed to make some pretence of searching for the letter, prolonging her futile rummaging long enough to give Teresa and her mother sufficient time to dispose of the subject of Mr. Fulroyd and his compositions.

As she came back through the hall she heard Jonathan Keyne's voice taking part in the present conversation and assumed thankfully that an entirely new topic was under discussion. But just outside the door she realised that this was not the case and, with no intention of really eavesdropping, she stopped dead in time to hear Teresa's clear, emphatic tones say,

"Mother, you're just being tiresome and arguing for the sake of argument. The fact is that the old man is a boring failure. It's just nonsense about these pretentious operas of his! They're no more than a joke in the district. He simply happens to be the local organist, but they're

74

not a seriously musical family – "

"The girl is," stated Keyne's voice coolly. "She has quite an exceptional voice."

"And what has she ever done with it, I'd like to know?" replied Teresa scornfully. "It's what you *do* with your possessions that establishes their value. A beautiful voice is no better than a beautiful piano until someone does something with it."

"Except that you can't buy a beautiful voice, whereas you can buy a beautiful piano," he answered with an amused note in his voice.

"All right. But *you* know better than almost anyone else how important the character and temperament are as well. That girl will never do anything much – take it from me – any more than her father. They've no real professional drive. They're essentially amateur in their approach."

"Well – " Keyne was laughing now and obviously not inclined to do real battle in the cause – "you may be right. I did have some reason to think her irresponsible, it's true, but – "

Anna slipped away before she could hear any more. She was hot with shame and cold with rage. And oddly enough, it was even more on her father's behalf than her own. How dared Teresa Delawney, who had never heard a note of her father's work, dismiss it as amateur? She didn't know anything about it!

Oh, of course it was true that those operas were unpractical – who knew that better than Anna and her mother? – but he was a musician to the very core of his being. While that stupid, spoiled *bossy* girl would never know what it was to love the great art of music as such.

She went back into the drawing-room. Where else could she go? For she could not face any of the three of them at the moment, and at least she had some sort of thin excuse for being here. She went and stood by the window, staring out across the terrace and gardens, unsuccessfully trying to hold back the angry tears which forced their way into her eyes. And presently she gave a muffled sob or two, not knowing if she were crying with rage or with a sort of anguished compassion for her father, who knew and felt so much but had never been able to express it in the art he longed to serve.

That was it. He was humbly willing to *serve* the great art of music. That wretched girl just wanted to use it to enhance her own prestige. And she presumed to speak disparagingly of him!

In an access of angry misery, Anna actually tore her slightly damp handkerchief across. And as she did so she realised that someone else had come into the room.

Some appalled sixth sense told her it was Jonathan Keyne, even before he came up behind her and said, "Good heavens! what's the matter?"

"Nothing." Even while she crumpled up the rags of her handkerchief in her hands she wished she could have thought of a slightly less idiotic reply.

He seemed to find it very silly, because he said coolly, "Well, that's a lie, anyway. And not a very clever one."

Then, to her boundless surprise, he took hold of her by her upper arms and turned her, gently but quite resistlessly, to face him.

"Come on, now, tell me what's wrong. Are you worried about your mother?"

"Oh, no, not now."

"Has someone been unkind to you?"

"N-no." The denial this time was not quite so emphatic, and suddenly she was tremendously aware of his strong, rather sensitive fingers holding her.

"Well then, I shall allow myself the proverbial third guess." He was laughing a little, but not unkindly. "You're upset because you're not singing in this Festival?"

"I'm not in the least!" At that moment she even thought that was true. "It's not me. It's my father!" And then suddenly the angry words came rushing out. "She had no *right* to brush him off like that. She doesn't know anything about it. She just – "

"If by 'she' you mean Teresa," he interrupted coolly, "it *is* her own special festival, you know."

"Oh, I know." All at once, Anna was horrified to realise how much she had said. "I don't know why I should mind so much. You must think me a perfect fool, but – "

"No, I don't." Unexpectedly he took his right hand away from her arm and actually touched her cheek with the back of his fingers "I think perhaps you agonise a bit too much about family loyalties. But that's rather a lovable fault, I suppose. Don't cry any more, Anna. I can't insist on your father being included in the Festival. After all, I don't know myself what his claims may be. But I'll try to get *you* included. How about that?"

If she had not been in quite such an emotional turmoil, or her family pride had been less bitterly hurt, she would probably have recognised this for a fair sized olive branch. As it was, however, it seemed to her altogether too much like offering a sweet to a child, and she cried scornfully,

"Thank you, but *I* don't want to be in this stupid Festival! I just thought how lucky they would be to get my father, but if they don't want him that's all right with me. As for my caring two pins about it – "

"Anna, stop being tiresome." He was still half laughing. "*I* want you to sing. Are you turning me down a

77

second time?"

"You – want me – ?" she stammered, staring up at him.

"If you look at me like that there's only one possible answer," he told her half seriously and, bending his head, he kissed her deliberately on the lips.

For a second she savoured some delicious emotion that was totally unfamiliar to her. Then, for some reason – perhaps the flicker of a movement – she looked past him, and saw that Teresa Delawney stood framed in the doorway, her eyes wide with fury as well as astonishment.

CHAPTER FOUR

"Oh, please – don't!" Panic-stricken at the sight of Teresa, Anna pushed Jonathan Keyne from her with more violence than she had intended, so that he released her with an angry exclamation and almost staggered back.

At the same moment Teresa moved away, so swiftly and silently that Anna stared for a moment at the empty doorway, almost thinking for a moment that she must have imagined the glimpse of that outraged figure. But she knew really that there was no imagination about it. Teresa had stood there all right, patently furious at the very idea that Jonathan should kiss anyone but herself.

Then, much too late, Anna turned to apologise to Jonathan Keyne, who had moved away and was standing by the piano, turning over some sheets of music which apparently absorbed his whole attention.

She came close to him and said with a nervous catch in her voice, "I'm sorry – I didn't mean – I was startled – " She broke off, aware suddenly that she could not possibly drag Teresa into the conversation as an explanation of her reaction. The whole incident was altogether too silly and undignified.

"Oh, don't apologise." He sounded rather scornfully amused. "I expect it's I who should do the apologising. I don't seem to have the right touch where you're concerned, do I? Forget it."

"But I assure you – "

"Please don't. Hollow assurances are always such a bore, aren't they?"

And, having crushed her effectually with that, he went

out of the room, leaving her divided between misery at having offended him again and acute anxiety about what Teresa might say to her when next they met.

On the latter account, however, there was no need to worry. Teresa made no reference whatever to what she had seen. Nor did she show any trace of resentment in her attitude to Anna. If anything, she was a trifle more cordial than usual, a circumstance which somehow disquieted Anna more than open enmity would have done. For she could not believe that she would not be made to feel the full weight of the other girl's displeasure eventually.

But it was not Teresa's way to put her anger into words. Her line was just to remove, with her customary efficiency, any undesirable element which stood in her path. That evening she telephoned home to Anna and explained, very plausibly and charmingly, that she would not be needing her for a few days as she was expecting important house guests.

"I shall be too much occupied with them, I'm afraid, to do much about the Festival. But I'll let you know when I need you again," she said.

"Which means that I shan't be asked back to Coppershaw Grange until Jonathan Keyne has safely returned to London – if then," Anna reflected. And it was no good telling herself that she didn't care. She cared very much indeed – to part once more from Jonathan Keyne on a note of misunderstanding, just as their relationship seemed likely to take a new and more friendly turn.

It was difficult not to be very unhappy during the ensuing week and, suddenly bereft of her truly interesting work, she began perversely enough to long for Coppershaw Grange on almost any terms, and to find her thoughts returning there again and again.

One day, in the main street, she met one of the maids from the Grange. She was on good terms with all the staff and the girl stopped to enquire after her.

"Aren't you coming to work at Coppershaw any more, Miss Fulroyd?" she asked.

"Oh, I hope so, Jenny. But at the moment Miss Delawney is too busy with other things to need me. I believe there are some important house guests, aren't there?"

Jenny nodded.

"Some famous conductor, they tell me," she said. "Friend of Mr. Keyne."

"Really?" Anna was interested. "What's his name?"

"I can't remember. Warren or something. Big chap with a rather la-di-da manner. But pleasant. He has a wife who sings."

"Oscar Warrender!" More intensely than ever did Anna regret being banished from the Grange at this time.

"Yes, that's the name," Jenny agreed. Then she nodded again in a friendly manner and went on her way.

But for the fact that this was the week when her mother was well enough to leave hospital and travel the twenty miles to the convalescent home, Anna would have had even more time to bemoan her ill-luck in missing all that was happening at the Grange. As it was, with relief and gratitude in her heart, she was able to accompany her mother and see her happily installed in the lovely country manor which housed the convalescent home.

"I'm going to miss seeing you every other day, of course," her mother said. "But how beautiful it is here!" And she looked out so contentedly at the wooded parkland that it was obvious that the thought of just lying there doing nothing was still uncharacteristically welcome to her. She was, Anna saw, going to take a long time to recover her customary strength and energy.

"I'll come whenever I can," Anna promised. "And so will Dad, of course."

"Don't let him neglect his work, though!" Her mother did speak with some energy then. "He's told me all about this song cycle he's doing for your Festival, and I wouldn't for the world have him miss that chance."

"N-no, of course not," Anna agreed. But she was somewhat taken aback to realise that apparently her father had been undeterred by any doubts she had subsequently cast on the possibility of the church concert taking place. It seemed he had just gone ahead on the assumption that his song cycle would certainly be included.

On the way home she tried worriedly to decide whether it would be kinder to damp down his hopes here and now, or more practical to let him go enthusiastically ahead. If the opportunity did in fact arise it would of course be most desirable that he should be fully prepared for it.

In the event, the choice was taken out of her hands. For no sooner had she reached home and reported satisfactorily on her mother's transfer to the convalescent home than her father said,

"Come along to the church in about an hour's time, Anna. I've been coaching young Tommy in the solo parts of the song cycle, and I want to take him over them now with the organ accompaniment."

She opened her lips to say that perhaps there would *be* no song cycle, at least so far as the Festival was concerned. But she decided suddenly that she simply could not be the one to quench that light of interest and happiness in her father's eyes. Besides, she was genuinely eager to hear for herself what Tommy Bream made of it, even without the choir. So far she had heard no more than snatches of the work on the piano or hummed a few lines herself.

So later she walked through the autumn twilight, carrying with her a duplicate copy of the words and manuscript of the music. It was almost dark when she reached the church, but her father had already put on a few lights, so that the beautiful fan vaulting was thrown into sharp relief, while alternating patches of light and shadow in the body of the church gave an almost mysterious air of peace and tranquillity to the scene.

As she took her seat in one of the middle pews her anxieties receded. It was going to be all right – it simply *had* to be all right – she told herself, as the first notes, the fine, clear, heart-lifting phrases connected with spring, floated through the church. The beautiful air which had so captivated her was stated right away in that first section, and Tommy's pure, clear voice sent it soaring up to the highest point of the vaulted roof.

It *was* beautiful! She had not been mistaken. Quite, quite beautiful, and the first impact was something astonishing. But then, as the work went on, she began to wonder if she sensed a gradual slackening of the tension. Tommy was singing well, and of course there would be more drama to the whole work when the choir was added. And yet – and yet – somehow it was not absolutely what she had expected.

She was tired, she told herself. Anxious about the final fate of the work. Not entirely in the right mood after being so concerned about her mother all day.

But that was not, she knew to the marrow of her bones, the complete answer to her dwindling enthusiasm. Could it possibly be that, after all, it was *not* the inspiration they had hoped? The mere possibility agitated her so unbearably that the pages of manuscript shook in her hands. For how was she – the sole audience on this occasion – to convey to her father either the enthusiasm she could not feel or the doubts she was trying to suppress?

And then suddenly she realised that she was not the sole audience. Someone who had been sitting at the back of the church had risen and was coming forward. She turned her head quickly and, to her immeasurable astonishment, she saw that Oscar Warrender was walking slowly down the centre aisle.

He came and sat down beside her and said in a low voice, "The boy is quite remarkable, but this work is not for him. Who is the organist?"

"My father," Anna told him shyly.

"And what is the work? It's quite unknown to me."

"He – he composed it. It's a song cycle. We were hoping that it might be performed during the Festival." Her words came out in a confidential rush. "But now – I don't know – "

"Yes, of course, it must be heard," was the astonishing reply. "But not with the boy. He must do Mendelssohn or Schubert or something like that. Have you the manuscript of this work there?" He indicated the pages she was holding and, without a word, Anna handed them to him.

He took them in his strong, expressive fingers and during the rest of the performance he said nothing more, merely studied the manuscript with close attention. At the end he said abruptly, "Introduce me to your father."

With the strange sensation of being in some sort of improbable dream, Anna followed him out of the pew and then led the way towards the choir stalls from which her father and Tommy Bream were now emerging.

"How did it sound to you, Anna?" Her father spoke eagerly before she could attempt any introductions.

"Very beautiful, so far as I could judge without the choir," she said nervously. "But – "

"It's not a work for a boy soprano, Mr. Fulroyd," stated Oscar Warrender with an air of absolute authority. "Good though he is." And he clapped Tommy on the shoulder with unexpected firmness, a gesture which suggested he knew a good deal about choirboys and the way their angelic looks belied their natural toughness. "It's a remarkable voice and, as I was telling your daughter, will sound splendid, I don't doubt, in Mendelssohn or Schubert or even Haydn perhaps. But this particular song cycle is for a *woman* soprano. Everything about it cries out for a female voice."

"My dear sir – " Mr. Fulroyd looked surprised and not a little incensed. "May I ask if you know anything about – "

"Dad, this is Mr. Warrender," exclaimed Anna urgently.

"I'm pleased to make your acquaintance, sir, since my daughter seems to know you. But, if I may so – "

"Mr. *Oscar* Warrender. The conductor." Anna amplified her first statement desperately.

"Well – " Then suddenly her father got the message of her words and tone. "Mr. Warrender, I do beg your pardon! I hadn't realised – "

"There's no need for apology. Your enquiry was completely in order. You are the composer of this unusual work, I understand. You were quite justified in querying anyone else's right to make suggestions."

"But from such a distinguished authority – "

"Never mind the mutual compliments." Suddenly Warrender gave his rare but very charming smile. Then he turned to Tommy Bream and said, "You can run along now, I think. I'd like to hear you again some time, but I want to talk with your choirmaster now."

Tommy withdrew – reluctantly because he scented some sort of drama in the air and would have liked to take part in it. Then, at a gesture from Warrender, Anna and her father sat down in the front pew, while he stood in front of them, in a perfectly natural attitude of authority, the manuscript copy of the song cycle still in his hands.

"Let me say right away – " he turned the pages consideringly – "that I find the work extraordinarily interesting and attractive. It is completely singable, for one thing. Something of a novelty in these days."

"Some people would say – a little old-fashioned," suggested Mr. Fulroyd deprecatingly.

"Possibly. But they would be wrong," replied Warrender with an almost careless confidence in his own judgment which put discussion out of the question. "There is no special fashion about it – in the sense of its being dated, I mean. But, as I said before, it is not for the passionless soprano of a choirboy. It is for a warm, brilliant lyric soprano, and I would say that the ideal exponent is sitting beside you."

"*Anna*, do you mean?" Mr. Fulroyd turned to look at his daughter, his eyes shining with interest and surprise. "I never thought of it! Perhaps one never does think of one's own child singing one's effusions." He laughed, that half shy laugh, and took off his spectacles and polished them diligently. "Anna! What a remarkable and delightful suggestion. At least, it is to me. How does the idea of your singing it appeal to you?"

"I'd adore to do it!" cried Anna.

Her father put his hand quickly over hers and then turned to the great conductor and asked curiously, "How do you happen to know that my daughter has the right voice for this work?"

"I heard her sing some weeks ago. I never forget a voice of quality," stated Oscar Warrender positively.

"And you think she has that?"

"I have no doubt of it, so far as the voice itself is concerned. And she is, I noticed, intensely musical. How much drive and power of concentration and application she may have I don't know."

"She is a dedicated worker," insisted Mr. Fulroyd without hesitation. "In a minor way I have been concerned with singers all my life, and I can truly say I have never known anyone more devoted to her art."

"Really?" The conductor's glance passed thoughtfully over Anna. "That was not the impression of my friend Jonathan Keyne."

"Then he was mistaken, sir," replied Anna's father with dignity.

"Possibly." Warrender looked amused, but not unkindly so. "The best of us have been so in our time. But – I was going to ask you – may I make a few further suggestions about this work of yours?"

"I should appreciate anything you have to say about it," said Mr. Fulroyd with sincerity, and his hand tightened instinctively on Anna's as it lay in her lap.

"Well, if I followed correctly, it is your idea that the cycle should start with the Spring section?"

"It is customary to regard that as the first season, isn't it?" Mr. Fulroyd said with a slight smile.

"I'm sure that was the Almighty's plan," agreed Warrender, and he smiled too in a dry way. "And even I wouldn't seek to improve on it in actual fact. But for the purposes of this particular work, I suggest you should plunge straight into the warmth and exuberance of high summer. There's nothing against that. Your opening chords are tremendously arresting and you have, I think – " he consulted the manuscript – "a particularly fine choral opening passage here."

"But it's a contradiction in terms," protested Anna's father. "I can't presume to alter the course of the seasons to suit my humble work."

"No. But you can enter the cycle of the seasons at any point you choose. Here, boldly stated, is the condition of full maturity. It is followed by the quite exquisite melancholy of decline in your autumnal scene – lovely bit for your middle voice here, Miss Fulroyd – and then the almost grim finality of winter, with those extraordinary bare phrases telling of life ebbing and virtually ceasing."

"Surely making the obvious ending?" interjected Anna's father.

"Not if you wish to send your audience away feeling uplifted and transported, Mr. Fulroyd. It is neither artistically – nor I think ethically – correct to give such finality to death. Both in the seasons and – " he glanced round the church – "I would suggest in this beautiful building, there is the absolute affirmation of returning life. The certainty of re-awakening. Of resurrection, if you prefer the term. Your spring section makes that claim in this strangely heart-lifting melody. It is of such perfect simplicity that it carries its own conviction. Believe me, that is the section which you should leave in the hearts and minds of your listeners."

Anna, who by now felt tears of happiness in her eyes – for never before had anyone spoken to her father like this – stole a glance at him and saw that he was regarding Warrender with something like awe as well as infinite pleasure.

"I never thought of it like that," he said slowly. "Mr.

Warrender, you're a genius."

"Oh, Dad, everyone knows that," muttered Anna uncomfortably.

"No, not everyone." The great conductor looked amused again. "I'm not absolutely sure of it myself, though I have my moments. But one thing I do know, Mr. Fulroyd. I recognise *real music* when I hear it. And that is what I have heard tonight. I congratulate you, and I beg you to revise the order of your work to some extent, and to let your daughter sing the solo part at the Festival."

"Nothing – but nothing would give me more pleasure!" cried Mr. Fulroyd, as he wrung Oscar Warrender's hand. "And I thank you more than I can say for your advice, which I shall follow to the letter."

"There's just one thing!" exclaimed Anna, hating to be the one to cast even a shadow of doubt on the glory of the moment. "It hasn't been actually decided that there should *be* a church concert at all during the Festival."

"Nonsense." Warrender brushed the protest aside as though it were a small and tiresome fly. "Of course there must be a church concert. With this work – composed by someone actually living in the festival district – and that boy soprano singing a well-chosen solo or two, it will be the highlight of the Festival."

"But – "

"Believe me, I know." He spoke quite pleasantly, but he gave Anna the glance which had been known to quell even the most stout-hearted of prima donnas.

"I don't doubt it, Mr. Warrender! and I wouldn't query your judgment for a moment. But – but it's Miss Delawney who will decide what will be performed at this Festival."

"Or Jonathan Keyne," retorted the conductor imperturbably.

"Or Jonathan Keyne," Anna agreed. "But I think," she added diffidently, "he will do what she wants."

"I wouldn't say it has gone as far as that," said Oscar Warrender, with an unexpected touch of humour. "But, in any case, I intend to hear that song cycle in this church, and I assure you it will be performed. All you and your father have to do is to ensure that the performance is as perfect as it can be." Then he glanced at his watch and said, "I must go. I'm driving to London tonight."

"So late?" exclaimed Anna's father.

"I prefer to drive through the night. Good-bye, Mr. Fulroyd. And don't just stop at this song cycle. It's too good to be only a flash in the pan, and I'd like to hear anything else you have done. Work hard, Miss Anna. A good performance is going to mean a lot to your father at this point."

And then he was gone, walking swiftly up the aisle and out at the centre door, and after a moment or two they heard the sound of a high-powered car being driven away.

Only then did Anna and her father relax from the sort of spell which had descended upon both of them. They looked at each other and she hugged him suddenly and exclaimed, "Did it really happen?"

"He said he wanted to hear more of my work. Oscar Warrender said that!" Mr. Fulroyd shook his head unbelievingly. Then on a note of happy urgency he added, "Anna dear, if you're not tired, what about our trying over one or two passages right away?"

So she came and stood near him in the choir stalls and sight-read, first of all the lovely autumnal air, with its almost nostalgic touch of recollection and resignation, and then the beautiful spring-time melody which spoke in terms of irrefutable simplicity of the indestructible life-cycle.

Her voice had been well rested recently, of course, though she had never neglected her daily practice, and it sounded fresh and brilliant, with a shimmering colour all its own. As the notes floated upward, and seemed to linger in the beautiful carved arches of the roof, Anna felt as though her soul lifted too. A sort of spiritual strength was generated within her, giving her the strange feeling that she could almost lift poor suffering humanity on the wings of her singing to something just a little beyond the mundane level of daily life.

At the end she glanced across at her father and saw that he was sitting at the organ with his head in his hands.

"Oh, Dad – " she went to him and touched his shoulder gently – "I know. It's almost unbearably lovely, isn't it?"

"I can't believe I wrote it." He looked up and wiped his glasses in that half-nervous way. "I simply don't know where it came from."

"Perhaps one never does know where it comes from when it's as lovely as that," she said gently. "But Mr. Warrender is so right. It's for a woman soprano, of course. It sounds quite different that way."

"And I'd never have known it if that dear, good man hadn't told me!"

It occurred to Anna that few people would have described Oscar Warrender as a dear, good man. But she thought he had made good his claim to that phrase that evening. So she said with genuine warmth,

"He's one of the few people who really do *know*. If he says it will be a success – it will."

"For you as well as for me," her father added, with a smile. "You sing it so beautifully, my dear. It's largely your singing which makes such a wonderful new thing of it. We must practise very thoroughly between now and the concert."

Again a tremor of anxiety passed through Anna at the thought that no one had yet confirmed that concert. But she felt it would be poor-spirited to say anything about that now. If Oscar Warrender felt confident about it, who was she to have doubts?

But she could not help wondering during the next day or two just how even Warrender was going to combat the bitter prejudice of Teresa Delawney. He could not have raised the subject with her personally, because he had driven straight off to London the same evening. Was he relying on persuading Jonathan Keyne to his viewpoint? and, through him, the jealous and dictatorial Teresa? If so, it seemed to Anna – particularly in her less optimistic moments – a rather frail line to cling to. Even with Warrender giving the orders.

And then she was summoned back to Coppershaw Grange.

Again the message came by telephone. Again Teresa's voice sounded disquietingly cordial. And again the assumption was that Anna would drop everything and come at once.

Anna dropped everything and went at once.

Teresa gave the impression of being in a friendly and expansive mood, and yet she volunteered none of the information which Anna was longing to have about what had happened at the Grange during her absence. Inevitably a good deal of work had accumulated, and Anna was expected to attend to this with all speed.

Mrs. Delawney was more casually informative, however. She liked Anna and said, apparently with sincerity:

"I wish you had been here during the last week. I

think it would have been specially interesting for you as a singer. Oscar Warrender was here. And his wife — Anthea Warrender, you know — came for a few days too. A charming couple."

"I'm sure they are," Anna agreed. "Did he have any suggestions to make about the Festival?"

"I believe he talked over a lot of things with Jonathan and Teresa. He's not professionally involved, as you know, only taking a friendly interest because he knows and likes Jonathan. But I think he felt they were making a good job of it. Anyway, he said he and his wife would be coming down for one or two of the principal events."

"Did he suggest any additions to the programme?" asked Anna carefully. For, after all, he *might* already have made some fresh suggestion by post or telephone.

But Mrs. Delawney shook her head consideringly.

"No, I don't think so." Then, going off at a tangent, she added, "You know, I'm really sorry myself that there is not to be a church concert. In my view, it would have been a splendid idea. I did bring up the subject again, but no one was specially enthusiastic. Indeed, Teresa seemed quite set against it. Very obstinate and silly of her, and I don't know why she should take up that attitude. But as it is in a way *her* festival, I suppose there's no more to be said. I hope you and your father are not too disappointed."

"No, of course not," Anna said as pleasantly as she could.

But to herself she thought, "That was before Oscar Warrender heard the song cycle. That made him change his mind. But he must say so — soon. What is he doing about it? The time is getting terribly short."

It was indeed. All the other arrangements had been confirmed and already there was mention in some of the national newspapers, as well as the local ones, of the interesting Festival which was to take place in the West Country.

Anna tried desperately to control her impatient anxiety, and to concentrate on putting all her heart and soul into perfecting her part in the song cycle. And when she sang it for the first time with full choir and organ she was so deeply impressed all over again that she felt it was impossible that it should not be heard as it deserved – in the framework of the Festival.

So far, on her urgent insistence, her father had not confided their high hopes to anyone else in his church circle, though a few whispers were going about among the choir members themselves. But most of them sang in the choir for the sheer joy of singing, and though they thought it exciting and novel to be doing something composed by old Fulroyd himself, and they were impressed by his daughter's voice, they were content to wait for whatever time might be judged suitable for a full-scale performance.

To Anna, the hardest part of all was to have to listen to her father's happy speculations about the final date, which – if any – of the London critics were likely to be there, and how the work would really go down on the great night. It was, she thought, so typically unrealistic of him not even to wonder why no definite details had even now been settled.

And then, one morning, something happened to switch her thoughts almost violently into a different channel.

Teresa, who had been wandering about the room and shifting a few things in an unusually restless manner, suddenly turned to her and said, as though impelled to speech,

"Anna, there's something I feel I ought to say to you — and I just don't know how to say it tactfully. Jonathan is coming down here again for a few days this week — "

She paused and Anna looked at her in astonishment and said, "Yes?" doubtfully.

"My dear, I know you're probably much too sensible to take him seriously when he turns on that twenty-two-carat-gold charm of his. But I wouldn't like you to get *hurt*, and so I think I should tell you that things are serious between him and me. I was afraid that if you thought he was unattached, you might — "

"I assure you, Miss Delawney — "

"Oh, not 'Miss Delawney', *please*! We've been Teresa and Anna for long enough, surely."

"Teresa, then," said Anna coldly. "There is not the slightest question of my — my taking any serious interest in Mr. Keyne. And really I resent your even suggesting such a thing."

"No, please don't resent what I said! Please, Anna dear. I've probably been tactless and clumsy. But I just didn't want you to get hurt," she insisted again.

"That's very thoughtful of you," replied Anna drily. "But there's no danger of that happening."

"Then that's all right. I'm so *glad*." And Teresa smiled her sweetest smile and went out of the room, closing the door carefully behind her.

Anna stared at the panels of the door and thought, "Liar! You blank, blank liar! A lot you cared about my being hurt. You weren't worrying about *me* — why should you, come to that? — you were just worrying about yourself and how securely you could get your hot little hands on Jonathan Keyne. And I don't believe he's serious about you anyway. At least — I don't think I do. And what does it matter if he is? He's nothing to me.

Absolutely nothing. Except for the fact that he kissed me in a way – "

She stopped and thought about the way he had kissed her. And then about the way Teresa had looked when she saw the scene. This latest move was simply her way of clearing the decks for action. Just as she had firmly eliminated the church concert from the Festival lest it should reflect credit and modest glory on Anna and her father, so she was reducing Anna to boring passivity so far as Jonathan was concerned.

But suppose Jonathan heard her sing in that song cycle – what then? If all went as Oscar Warrender seemed to think it would go, he would see her in a very different light. He *must*! For once she would triumph happily and bask in his astonished interest and approval.

Only how was that to be brought about unless someone took a hand and forced the issue? What was Warrender doing? – what was *anyone* doing to see that the concert took place? Nothing. Just exactly nothing. It must be that in the press of his many other commitments Oscar Warrender had forgotten the absolute necessity of his intervening. And now each day made it less and less likely that anything could be done. It was not as though she could do anything herself –

And then at that moment the telephone rang beside her.

She stared resentfully at the thing, not wanting to speak to anyone. But self-discipline reasserted itself and she picked up the telephone, to find that there was a call from London, from the national newspaper which always made a special point of noticing musical events of any real importance.

"Can I speak to Miss Delawney, please?" asked the voice at the other end.

"Miss Delawney has just gone out, I'm afraid," said Anna, watching through the window Teresa's car shooting off down the drive. "I'm her secretary. Can I help you?"

"Well, perhaps you could. We are doing a special feature about this festival which Miss Delawney is organising. It has a rather unusual angle, with the family background and Jonathan Keyne being involved, and I believe Oscar Warrender even is taking some interest in it and will be present part of the time?"

"Yes, that is all correct," Anna agreed.

"We wondered if there were anything else rather special – anything not yet mentioned – that we might enlarge upon. Something with particular local significance, for instance."

Anna felt a great lump rise in her throat, choking her into silence for several seconds.

Then the voice went on – "I may as well tell you there is a rumour going about that there is to be some sort of surprise at this festival. Is that correct?"

"Where did you get that story?" Anna asked cautiously.

"Oh, by the general grapevine, you know. Any comment?"

There was, of course, no comment whatever which she was entitled to make. And yet – only a few minutes ago – she had been brooding angrily on the desperate necessity for someone's hand to be forced.

Suddenly, in the clearest detail, she saw what she could do. And because she was so agonisingly sick of inaction, so wretchedly aware of the grains of sand that were slipping through Time's hourglass, she spoke with calm directness, hardly a tremor in her voice.

"Don't quote me personally, will you? But if you want an exclusive piece of news – yes. The highlight of the

Festival is going to be a church concert, as yet un-announced. There is, as the special attraction, the world premiere of a song cycle, composed by the local organist and very highly thought of by Oscar Warrender. It is for soprano, choir and organ."

"You don't say!" There was no doubting the interest generating at the other end of the line. "Boy soprano?"

"No, it's for a woman – lyric soprano."

"That sounds very interesting."

"Yes, we're all rather excited about it," said Anna, wondering if she had gone mad.

"Who is singing the soprano part? Not Anthea War-render?"

"Oh, no, no one as famous as that. The part is to be sung by the composer's daughter, Anna Fulroyd."

"Anna Fulroyd? I seem to know that name. Didn't she have some rather favourable mention recently from one or two of the London critics?"

"I believe she did," agreed Anna coolly.

"Well, that's really quite a story! Just the sort of per-sonal touch we wanted. Thank you very much." And the line went dead.

"Don't mention it," said Anna into the silence. Then she replaced the receiver and sat staring at the wall in front of her.

CHAPTER FIVE

THERE are some people – usually with a gambling streak in them – who can take all sorts of risks, live through them without too much anguish, and accept philosophically whatever the final outcome may be. But Anna was not one of these.

The moment she had staked her all on forcing Teresa's hand with regard to the church concert she was overwhelmed with horror at what she had done. It was true that she had some reason to think of Oscar Warrender as being on her side. But he was far away in London, whereas Teresa was very much here, believing in her more or less divine right to direct everything to do with the Festival.

"I did tell the man not to quote me personally," Anna thought miserably. "But I couldn't expect him to hold to that if Teresa herself queried the truth of his statements."

For a black moment or two she even wondered if her best course would be to make a frank confession to Teresa when she returned. But that seemed a pretty poor-spirited way of following up her bid for justice. Perhaps if she brazened it out –

She had never felt less brazen in her life. On the other hand, since she had taken that first mad, irrevocable step, there would be neither sense nor dignity in rushing to embrace defeat even before it overtook her. It was just remotely – oh, so remotely! – possible that even Teresa might prefer to accept the hated concert rather than turn unsought (but valuable) publicity into a farcical denial.

Whichever way it went, of course, Teresa would never forgive her. Nor would Jonathan Keyne, probably, come to that. Certainly not if he were as deeply involved with Teresa as she made out. Not, Anna assured herself, that she cared in the least what either of them thought. And if this were not the whole truth, it was half of it. The half that related to Teresa, that was to say.

During the rest of the day she managed to preserve a fairly cool demeanour, concentrating hard on her work lest her agitated thoughts should lead her into any serious error. If she could not bring herself to say much to Teresa – nor even to look her full in the face – no doubt this was put down to embarrassment following on the conversation about Jonathan that morning.

Teresa, for her part, was unusually gracious – complimenting Anna on her work and announcing that of course she would be expected as a guest at the Eighteenth Century party which would end the Festival. But graciousness is a quality which exalts the dispenser and diminishes the recipient, and Anna went home depressed and dispirited beyond description.

In contrast, she found her father in excellent spirits and eager to discuss with her the final form of the projected concert.

"Dad, I hate to be a wet blanket," she said desperately at last, "but there may not *be* a church concert during the Festival. Don't you realise that even now Teresa Delawney hasn't made any statement confirming it? And the final decision rests with her."

"But why haven't you asked her outright?" Mr. Fulroyd looked astonished. "I thought you were on such friendly terms."

"No, I wouldn't describe us exactly as that," murmured Anna uncomfortably. "She was nice about sending fruit and flowers to Mother, of course, and she always seems satisfied with my work, but – "

To her surprise, her father laughed unexpectedly and patted her reassuringly on the shoulder.

"Then perhaps I know more about it than you do," he said good-humouredly. "I had a telephone call from London this afternoon, from the *Daily Echo*. They knew all about the concert, and the song cycle. They even knew that you were to be the soloist and they wanted some personal details. If Miss Delawney hasn't given them all this information, who else has?"

Who indeed?

Anna stared at her father for a moment in consternation, feeling like someone who had wilfully lit a very, very small bonfire, only to see it burst into a great conflagration. But apparently her father took her wide-eyed expression to be no more than surprise at his interesting news, for he said contentedly, "You'll see. Everything is going to be all right."

There seemed little to add to that. So Anna smiled faintly and was silent.

The next morning she rushed down early, almost before the newspaper was thrust through the letterbox. But though she searched through the *Daily Echo* feverishly, to her mingled relief and disappointment there was nothing about Teresa's Festival. She was obviously going to have to wait another day – or two or even three – before the blow fell. Meanwhile, there was nothing to do but go to the Grange as usual and get through her day's work, her heart in her mouth every time the telephone rang or Teresa came into the room.

Early in the afternoon Jonathan Keyne and Roderick Delawney arrived, almost at the same moment. They had both motored down from London, neither realising that the other was coming, and virtually met on the door-step.

"Oh, Jonathan, how glad I am to see you!" Teresa's welcoming kiss was distinctly less casual than before, Anna thought. "There are so many things to work out, and I've missed all your professional know-how."

He laughed and declared she was well able to manage the Festival single-handed, but was not displeased, Anna saw, to be appealed to as the final authority. His greeting to Anna was polite rather than warm. But Rod – who came into the room a few minutes after him, accompanied by Mrs. Delawney – greeted Anna before he even addressed his sister.

And what he said was, "Congratulations, Anna! I see you're to sing in the Festival after all."

There was a moment of stunned silence. Then Anna stammered, "Wh-where did you hear that?"

At almost the same moment Teresa exclaimed scornfully, "She certainly is not! What gave you that idea?"

"My copy of the *Daily Echo*, in which I have more or less implicit faith," retorted her brother amusedly. "It's all here – " he produced his copy of the newspaper in question – "Song Cycle by Mr. Fulroyd, local organist – soloist his own daughter – to be the highlight of the Festival, if Oscar Warrender is to be believed and – "

"You must be mad! *They* must be mad!" His sister was white with barely controlled rage. "There's not a word of truth in it. And there's nothing about it in *my* paper."

"You take the wrong paper," replied her brother, laughing.

"Don't be a fool! It's no laughing matter. I mean that it's not in my copy of the *Echo*."

"That's the worst of these provincial editions." Rod

102

was rather unfairly enjoying himself. "You'll get it in yours tomorrow, I expect. Mine is the latest London edition, of course."

"But it's not true! It's not *true!*" Suddenly Teresa's composure broke and she turned on Anna in undisguised fury. "*You* must have done this – you and your father! You cooked it up between you, thinking you'd force your way in. You little snake – "

"Teresa!" her mother spoke sharply.

"Don't 'Teresa' me! I'll say what I like about my own Festival. No one else could have given such a story to the papers. And anyway, you have only to look at her! She looks sick with guilt and fright."

"She looks pale with shock and surprise, you mean," interjected Jonathan Keyne very coolly. "The person who gave that story to the *Echo* was Oscar Warrender."

"Oscar Warrender?" said everyone, including Anna, in accents of profound astonishment. And then Teresa added unsteadily, "What could Warrender know about it? What do *you* know about it, come to that?"

"Rather more than you, it seems." Jonathan Keyne still spoke very coolly indeed. "Perhaps you'd like to apologise to Anna, and then she might tell us how Warrender came to know anything about her father's song cycle."

"How did he know?" Teresa turned to Anna again, but much less aggressively this time.

"No, my dear. First things first," interrupted Jonathan, putting a hand rather firmly on Teresa's shoulder.

"What do you mean?" she glanced back quickly at him.

"We all realise you're under a great strain about this Festival of yours, but – " he nodded his head slightly in Anna's direction, and after a moment Teresa said reluctantly,

"I'm sorry, Anna. It was the – the shock. How did Warrender come to know anything about all this?"

"He came into the church on his last evening here." Anna avoided Jonathan Keyne's interested glance and spoke in a low, rather husky voice. "My father was playing the organ and Tommy Bream was singing the soprano part of this – this song cycle my father had composed. Mr. Warrender was very deeply impressed, and he said it ought to be included in the Festival. But he told my father it was a work for a female soprano rather than a choirboy, and he – he gave it as his opinion that I had the right voice for the part."

"Good for him!" interjected Rod Delawney.

But his sister gave him a quelling glance and asked Anna coldly, "How did Oscar Warrender know what sort of voice you had?"

"We both auditioned Anna a month or two ago," stated Jonathan before she could speak.

"And he remembered the voice?" Teresa's tone somehow conveyed the idea that Anna was totally unmemorable in every way.

"He was kind enough to say – " Anna tilted up her chin suddenly and looked proudly at Teresa – "that he never forgot a voice of quality."

"Nor, incidentally, do I," murmured Jonathan with a touch of amusement in his expression. And Anna, watching, thought Teresa took this badly.

"But how perfectly splendid!" At this moment Mrs. Delawney looked up from the *Daily Echo* which she had been reading with the utmost attention. "Why, Teresa, it's much the best write-up we've had so far. We've had put right on our plate, as you might say, the world premiere of a work by a local composer which has already won praise from Oscar Warrender. And for soloist we have a singer who also belongs to the district. *Any* festival might be proud to present such an interesting combination. I always *said* we ought to have a church concert!"

"And I said not," retorted her daughter, allowing pique to override her better judgment.

"Well, you were wrong, dear," replied Mrs. Delawney unmoved. "I appeal to Jonathan, who knows more about these things than any of us. Wouldn't it be stupid to refuse this chance now?"

"I don't see how you *can* refuse it, Mrs. Delawney, even if it were desirable to do so. This sudden fanfare of publicity, thanks to – " his glance passed over Anna – "Warrender, pretty well forces us to put on the discussed work. And anyway, why look a gift horse in the mouth?"

"Warrender could be mistaken," said Teresa shortly.

"He seldom is. Besides, what have you against such a concert, Teresa? especially as it would have several features which couldn't fail to give interest and novelty to the whole Festival."

"I don't like to be stampeded into something I haven't thought out in detail for myself," replied Teresa, and for a moment her hard but beautiful eyes met Anna's with a dislike she could not conceal. "I know Warrender is a great man and all that. But no one else has heard this song cycle – "

"The choir all like it," Anna volunteered quickly.

"Oh, the *choir*! What do they know? All choirs think anything their choirmaster does is wonderful. I meant that none of *us* have heard it."

"You could remedy that this evening," replied Anna, and again that little proud lift of the head transformed her into an artist rather than Teresa's runabout. "The choir will be there for practice anyway. And I'll come if you want to hear me."

"What a good idea!" That was Mrs. Delawney, speaking before her daughter could. "How about you, Jonathan? Would you be available?"

"Of course."

"And nothing would keep me away," declared Rod. "Shouldn't Anna call it a day so far as work is concerned, if she's going to undertake an important piece of singing tonight?"

"She certainly should," agreed Jonathan. "Get your coat, Anna, and I'll drive you down home now."

As on a previous occasion, both Teresa and her brother tried to query this arrangement, but Jonathan refused to be overruled, saying firmly that he would take the opportunity to look in once more at the church.

"If we're going to make a great feature of this particular concert, perhaps we should let the Press have photographs of the church. It's an unusually beautiful setting, if I remember rightly."

"It is indeed," agreed Mrs. Delawney with a satisfied smile, for, like her daughter, she also liked to have her own way.

In silence Anna went out to the car with Jonathan, and in silence they drove as far as the gate. Then, as they turned into the lane which led from the Grange to the main road, he said, looking straight ahead, "May I now ask the sixty-four-thousand-dollar question?"

"Which is – what?" she enquired rather faintly.

"Who did give all that information to the *Daily Echo*?"

"You said yourself – it was Oscar Warrender," she exclaimed defensively.

"But it wasn't. I know that."

"*How* do you know?"

"Because he told me all about it last night and said he

relied on me to persuade Teresa that this church concert could be the sensation of the Festival. He was relying on *me* – he wasn't giving any story to the newspapers. That isn't Warrender's way, anyway."

"Then why did you say he had done it, if it wasn't true?"

He shrugged and laughed in a half vexed way.

"Shall we say that I'm not a hunting man, and so I don't like to see the fox – much less a little vixen – thrown to the hounds?"

There was a short pause. Then she said, "All right, *I* told them. Thank you for not giving me away."

"Whatever made you do it, Anna?" There was real interest in his voice. "I didn't know you had it in your make-up. Actually to force Teresa's hand like that."

"It was a sudden impulse. I'm ashamed about it now, but – "

"No, don't be! Many an armour-plated prima donna would envy you your tactics. I begin to think you really might make a success of things now."

She gave a half shocked little laugh.

"It may have been ingenious, but it was a bit un-scrupulous," she admitted. "It was mostly because of my father, I think. It is perfectly true that Mr. Warrender was impressed with his work. No one had ever spoken to my father like that before. He – my father, I mean – looked as though the heavens had opened and the angels had sung his praises. He had almost lost faith in himself – and suddenly Mr. Warrender restored it. And he promised that the song cycle should be heard at the Festival."

"He had no authority for doing so," Jonathan interjected, "but then Warrender wouldn't worry about that, of course."

"He made several marvellous suggestions to make the

song cycle more effective, and my father couldn't have been better pleased if Mozart himself had looked over his shoulder and given him a few hints. Then Mr. Warrender went away and my father just had no doubt at all that his song cycle would be heard at the Festival."

"But you did have a few doubts?"

"Mr. Keyne—"

"The name is Jonathan," he interjected unexpectedly.

"Is it?" She smiled faintly. "Does that mean that I'm coming up a bit in your estimation from the tiresome bore you once thought me?"

"You're not doing badly," he said. "Go on with your story."

"Well, I waited and waited, knowing that — that Teresa was very set against any thought of a church concert."

"Not actually set against it, Anna. Don't exaggerate, even if you're feeling rather sore about Teresa at the moment. She just didn't visualise a place in the Festival for that sort of concert."

Anna silently reserved judgment, but had the good sense not to argue.

"Anyway, I was getting a bit panicky, because I saw time was getting short, and I knew that my father had all his hopes and joy pinned on the performance of his work. And then, suddenly, the *Daily Echo* telephoned yesterday and asked for what they called an interesting story in connection with the Festival. So" – again she made that proud, defiant little movement of her head – "I *gave* them an interesting story."

He laughed at that, and she thought she caught an odd little note of admiration in the laugh.

"And now, this evening, you've got to prove yourself to us all," he said, half teasingly.

"I'm not afraid. At least, I'm not afraid of you."

"Why not of me?"

"Because, though you've been rather horrid to me once or twice, I think you're absolutely fair when it comes to your artistic judgment."

"*Have* I been rather horrid to you once or twice?" he asked, as he stopped the car in front of her house, and he sounded very slightly nettled as well as amused.

"Yes. But it wasn't entirely your fault," she conceded generously. "A friend of mine always says one has to have luck as well as everything else, and I haven't been lucky in my encounters with you. I've always somehow put myself in a bad light. Behaving stupidly about the audition because I was distracted with worry about my mother. And then pushing you away that time you – you – "

"When I kissed you," he finished for her. "I'd have said it was *my* luck that was out that time. You nearly knocked me over in your efforts to repulse me. I'd no idea you packed such a punch."

"Nor had I," she admitted, and suddenly, for the first time, they were laughing in friendly unison, and it was quite easy for her to say, "Teresa was standing in the doorway, and I hardly thought she would like the idea of her part-time secretary flirting with her house guests."

"The devil! Was that what it was?"

"That was what it was," Anna agreed, and she wondered now why she could not at the time have put the whole incident on this half-laughing level.

"I'm sorry, Anna." He turned and put his arm along the back of the seat. "Sorry that the luck was out both times, I mean. But – " he smiled at her suddenly – "one can always create a second time. If one wants to sufficiently."

"I – suppose so, yes." She glanced down at her clasped hands as they lay there in her lap. "If one wants to sufficiently."

"The second chance of an audition is coming up tonight, Anna, isn't it? Will you sing specially for me when you sing in your father's song cycle tonight?"

She nodded without answering.

"And as for the other occasion – allow me a second chance for that too." And, leaning forward, he kissed her softly on her cheek.

She did recall quite clearly at that moment what Teresa had said about his twenty-two-carat-gold charm, but it didn't seem to have any special significance. Nothing seemed to have any real significance except the fact that he had kissed her. And so she leaned across and returned the kiss – not on his cheek, because he turned his head at the exact moment that she leaned forward, so that their lips met and they kissed each other full on the mouth.

"Thank you, darling," was the astonishing thing he said. "It was a lovely second chance. And now you must run along in and rest. If you want to practise at all don't overdo it. I want to hear that beautiful voice of yours tonight in all its individual freshness."

She supposed afterwards that she got out of the car, crossed the pavement and went into the house with some air of normality. But, so far as her recollection went, she floated on clouds of gold, and if she had gone straight through the door without having to open it she would not have been entirely surprised. It would just have been all one with the magic of the moment when the whole world changed because Jonathan Keyne had kissed her and called her "darling".

Her father was not yet in, but a dazed glance at the clock told her that he would be home in less than half an hour. That gave her a few precious moments to stand there in the centre of the room, her hands pressed to her eyes, while she savoured the full joy of being friends with Jonathan again.

Well, not even *again*. For she never had been real friends with him. In the early days she had been no more than a candidate for audition. After that she had almost immediately become first the ungrateful creature who had thrown his marvellous offer back in his face and then the absurdly offended girl who had crushed him for impertinence when he had been teasing and admiring her.

"But we both laughed about it together at last!" she thought happily. "We both thought it funny. Not a matter for friction and misunderstanding, but for shared amusement. And he kissed me – *really* kissed me. I don't believe a word Teresa said! Not about their meaning something special to each other, nor about his charm being dangerous. Oh, he *has* charm of course – loads of it. But it's real, not just put on to dazzle people. And he said I was to sing specially for him tonight. I will, I will! I'll sing as I never sang before, and Dad's beautiful music will enchant them all. But most of all Jonathan. Oh, dear clever Mr. Warrender, to suggest that *I* should sing it. I could almost love him too just for thinking of that."

When her father came in she was at the piano, running over a specially difficult passage in the final section of the work. But she jumped up and embraced him and cried,

"They're all coming to hear the rehearsal tonight! All the Delawneys – except Mr. Delawney, of course. I don't think he's interested in anything but stocks and shares. But Jonathan Keyne will be there, and it's got to be better than it's ever been before, Dad. Jonathan Keyne is coming specially to hear me – us, I mean. And although

Teresa is still resistant to the idea of a church concert, she's going to be overruled because – "

"But if she's resistant to the idea of a church concert," interrupted Mr. Fulroyd bewilderedly, "why did she give all that information to the newspaper?"

"She didn't. I did," replied Anna succinctly.

"*You* did, Anna? But with what authority?"

"None. It was my own private little stroke of genius," said Anna, who by now was really rather flown with her own part in things.

Her father, however, was scandalised.

"Do you mean that you gave all that story when in fact the organiser of the Festival had not even decided to have such a concert?"

Anna nodded defiantly.

"But, my dear, that was completely unethical!"

"Of course it was. But so are most of the things Teresa Delawney does. You have to fight people with their own weapons sometimes."

"You know perfectly well that's a most specious line of argument," said her father severely. "And I'm ashamed to hear you use it."

"Well, not everyone thinks as you do," said Anna hastily. "Jonathan Keyne himself said that many an armour-plated prima donna would envy me my tactics."

"Possibly so. They're an unscrupulous lot, I understand, when it comes to cutting each other's throats. But I don't like the idea of *your* doing such things."

"Oh, all right, Dad. I felt guilty about it at the time, if you want to know. But there was some pretty dirty work on the other side and – Oh, I'll explain it all another time," she cried, seeing further bewilderment on her father's face and greatly fearing that they would be splitting hairs for the next fifteen minutes if she didn't take a firm stand. "It's all right, darling. Truly it is! At least, it's going to be after tonight. Don't think of anything but the rehearsal. It's got to be SUPERB."

"Very well." Unable to resist her happiness and enthusiasm, her father smiled – still rather doubtfully – and consented to being hustled through a light meal and then a few minutes of practice. Neither of them really required the latter, for both knew every note and musical nuance of the work which had occupied their thoughts and hopes for so long. But, like most artists, Anna liked to "sing herself in" before any performance of importance. And this, she felt, was to be one of the most important performances of her life.

Then they went down to the church, and Mr. Fulroyd explained to the choir that they must all do better than their best that evening, because they would be more or less on trial for inclusion in the Festival programme.

Tommy Bream at this point accidentally – at least, he said it was accidentally – released his pet white mouse among the ladies of the choir and there was quite a scene. But order was presently restored, the mouse – returned once more to its cage – was taken out into the vestry, and Tommy's voice was already soaring in angelic tones in the first anthem when the party from the Grange arrived.

From where she was sitting Anna could not see individually who was there, but it seemed to her that the Delawneys must have gathered some of their friends to accompany them, for there was quite a group of them. Mrs. Delawney came first, slightly ahead of the others and, with a gracious little gesture to Mr. Fulroyd, indicated that the rehearsal should proceed without any interruption on their account.

So Tommy – whose faultless soprano had not so much as quavered, in spite of his interest in the visitors – completed his anthem and sat down, looking as though he were justifiably expecting the Pearly Gates to open for him at any moment.

Then there was a slight rustle among the choir, as they stood up, their manuscript copies of the song cycle in their hands. A nod from Mr. Fulroyd, a few opening chords on the organ, and they burst into the quite splendid chorus with which the Summer section opened.

To Anna it had never sounded better. And, although she could not actually see Jonathan from where she was sitting in the choir stalls, she thought she could somehow sense the impression which the work must be making upon him from the outset.

When she herself stood up to sing she was almost glad that she could not see him. Thus there was nothing and nobody – not even Jonathan – to distract her attention from the joy and beauty of what she was singing. She could hear her own voice, mounting triumphantly against the rich background of the choral singing, and during the slight pause before the next section of the work she was aware of a stirring of interest and a murmur of approval among the group who had come with the Delawneys. Even Teresa smiled slightly when her mother leaned across and said something to her.

And then Anna's full attention was back again on the work, and she was preparing for her long solo depicting the beautiful melancholy of Autumn. This called for fine, well-supported legato singing, and she unconsciously called on everything that Madame Marburger had taught her over the years. She was hardly even nervous. Just on her mettle and determined to do herself and her teacher credit.

The short, fateful Winter section was almost completely choral, and then came the fine flower of the work – the hopeful, tender, and then radiantly confident promise of returning life and Spring. If it had been intentionally written for Anna's voice it could hardly have shown her off better. And, by that peculiar but indefinable process of communication between artist and artist, she knew that the choir, in tribute, were singing their very best too, happy and proud to supply the beautifully harmonised support for the ever-soaring melody.

At the end, ignoring the fact that they were in church, one or two of the visitors actually applauded. Then Mrs. Delawney, followed by most of her party, came forward to congratulate Anna and her father and the gratified choir.

"It's a quite wonderful work," exclaimed one of the men. "I only wish *I* had written it!"

And Mrs. Delawney, introducing him to Anna's father, said, "This is Marcus Bannister, who composed 'The Exile', you know." Whereupon the two men fell into animated talk, and Mrs. Delawney drew forward the girl who had accompanied Bannister and said to Anna,

"I think Gail Rostall wants to tell you herself how much she enjoyed your singing."

"I do indeed!" The other girl smiled at Anna and added, "You must surely be a pupil of Elsa Marburger? I think only she could have – "

"I am, I am!" Anna was only too happy to pay tribute to her teacher. "I needed to call on everything she ever taught me in that Autumn section."

"That was where I felt sure you were a pupil of hers. Do tell me – " and for several minutes they eagerly discussed their teacher and the way in which she had helped them both.

It was such a delight and refreshment to Anna to be talking again of the art which was her life that she scarcely noticed anyone else. Even Jonathan had momentarily retreated into the background of her consciousness. But then someone else claimed Gail Rostall's attention, and Anna was once more seized upon by the triumphant Mrs. Delawney.

"Warrender was right – as always, of course. This will be the sensation of the Festival. We have just enough time to advertise it worthily. And Jonathan must see to it that – "

"Where *is* Mr. Keyne, incidentally?" interrupted Anna. And with a sudden chill, so nearly physical that she actually trembled, she took in fully the fact that *he* had not come near her to offer either congratulation or comment.

"Oh, in the end, he didn't come – " began Mrs. Delawney, and then someone caught her by the arm and asked a question about the church, and she was only too pleased to speak at length on what was one of her favourite subjects.

He hadn't come!

He had kissed her and asked her to sing specially for him that evening. And she had done so, with all her heart and soul and voice. And he had just not bothered to come.

For a moment Anna stood there, silent and half stunned. Then suddenly she saw that Teresa was watching her. And because, even in this fearful moment she felt the remnants of her pride stirring, she went over to the other girl and asked boldly,

"How did *you* like the work, Teresa?"

"Enormously." Teresa spoke with every appearance of generous candour. "I was wrong and Mother was right. The work is fine and you sing it beautifully. It can't fail to be a success."

If she had been a good friend she could not have said

more. And the unexpectedness of her reaction rocked Anna on her heels. Perhaps that was why it was to Teresa, of all people, that she put the burning question,

"Why didn't Mr. Keyne come?"

"Oh, he had an important phone call from London at the last minute and felt he should deal with that instead," Teresa explained carelessly, as she turned away. Then she looked over her shoulder and added, "He said to tell you he was sorry he couldn't make it."

CHAPTER SIX

He was sorry he couldn't make it! That was all. He was just sorry he could not make it.

For a moment it seemed to Anna that there was nothing and no one in the church except herself and her pain and fury and misery. Before she had had time to savour it fully, her artistic triumph was dust and ashes, and the remembrance of Jonathan's lips on hers a bitter taste that nothing would ever sweeten. She had been an utter, utter fool.

Teresa had been right when she told her not to take Jonathan seriously. She should have listened to Teresa – bitterest thought of all! That charm, that whimsical friendliness had not meant a thing. He had asked her to sing specially for him, and she had done so. And all the time he had not even bothered to be there.

She had to call on all her self-control and pride to live gracefully through the next twenty minutes. She thought the talk and jubilation would never end. Roderick Delawney in particular could not say enough about his delight in her triumph.

"I knew all along that you ought to be in this Festival," he declared. "I felt it in my bones, even though you were so modest and retiring about your qualifications."

"You were just guessing." Anna forced a smile. "You didn't really know anything about me as an artist."

"Except that you had the loveliest speaking voice, in addition to that *something* which makes one want to know more about you. I suppose it's what people mean by personality. Anyway, it got me, right from that first day when I saw you standing there in the wind and rain, and you let me drive you to the hospital."

"You were so kind to me that time," murmured Anna, wondering how much longer she would have to go on making this sort of conversation, while all the time she wanted only to rush away and cry on her own, and rage against Jonathan Keyne.

"I wasn't being kind. I was pleasing myself," Rod told her with some emphasis. "I don't think you know how appealing and forlorn you looked on that windswept platform."

"Oh, not *now*!" thought Anna. "I just can't take drippy compliments at this moment."

But then he had indeed been kind, and it was ungrateful to feel irritated just because his timing was bad. So she let him go on talking to her and she somehow managed to carry the burden of her part in the conversation, until suddenly there was a moment's pause and she could ask, in an almost natural voice,

"Why didn't Jonathan Keyne come to hear this rehearsal? I thought he was dead keen on hearing – the work."

"He was. I think he was fed up at not being able to come. But he was phoned for from London. His grandfather died suddenly, it seems."

His grandfather! It was ludicrous in its almost comic form of insult. Like the standard stories of the office boy asking for the day off "to bury his grandmother".

"Was he so devoted to his grandfather?" she heard herself ask rather coldly.

"I shouldn't think so," Rod said indifferently. "One of the toughest old tycoons who ever planned a tricky merger, I'd say. He even bested my father once, and that takes some doing. Not that there were any hard feelings about it. They respected each other, being birds of a feather. Though buzzards, as you might say, rather than larks. That's how Jonathan came to be a friend of the family."

"I see," said Anna.

But she didn't really see at all. She could see no good or proper reason why Jonathan should not have put off his journey for an hour or two, so that he could come and hear her on that one vital occasion when he had asked her to sing specially for him.

It was over at last. All the congratulations and good wishes and discussion. And even Teresa seemed so relaxed and good-humoured that she was talking quite gaily to Anna's father.

"We'll make the concert on the Tuesday of the second week, Mr. Fulroyd. We need a high spot of interest just then, because the impetus of the first week will just be slackening. Would you submit a programme to me in the next day or two, and I'll let you know within twenty-four hours if it's approved or requires further discussion. Though after tonight, I feel I can safely leave things to you."

And she smiled so charmingly at him that, as Anna and he walked home together under what seemed to her to be a cold and indifferent moon, he said,

"Miss Delawney is really a very sympathetic and knowledgeable young woman, after all. I hadn't realised that. It just shows how mistaken one can be about people."

How mistaken indeed!

Not until they were actually in the house did Mr. Fulroyd think to enquire, "What happened to Jonathan Keyne? I thought he was coming specially to hear you in the song cycle this evening?"

"He was." She tried not to choke on that. "But his grandfather died suddenly and he had to go to London."

She wondered if that sounded as idiotic to her father as it did to her. But apparently not, because he simply said, "Dear me, that's too bad. But he will hear you at the actual concert, no doubt. I must say, Anna dear, you were quite wonderful. You never sang better in your life."

"And I never shall again," she thought unhappily. "*Everything* was there to make me give of my best. Or I thought it was. I can't imagine my ever again feeling so gloriously uplifted and inspired."

Fortunately, she recognised this in a moment or two as the ultimate depths of contemptible self-pity, and she pulled herself back just in time, with the bracing reflection that she had managed to sing very well before Jonathan Keyne came along, and would no doubt do so again. But, unlike every other form of artist, a singer is his or her own instrument. And what happens to the singer is almost invariably reflected in the voice. Of *course* she had sung with radiant joy and a conviction in the reality of happiness. That was the way she had felt – when she believed that Jonathan was listening eagerly to her. It was going to be difficult to recreate that mood now that she knew how little she really meant to him.

Worn out with excitement and effort – and disappointment, Anna slept deeply, but she woke to a sense of depression. Her father, in contrast, was in splendid spirits at breakfast time. He had no reason to be otherwise. It was she who had to put on a convincing pretence of regarding the previous evening as one of the highlights of her life.

She was almost glad to get away at last, even though it meant going to Coppershaw Grange where she would have to pretend once more, though in a slightly different way. For, whatever happened, Teresa must never, never know what a blow had been dealt her when she discovered that Jonathan had not even bothered to come and hear her.

It was easier than her fears had prompted her to expect, for Teresa was much occupied with the Bannisters. Gail naturally wanted to see the Tithe Barn, which had now been converted into a very attractive countrified little theatre, since it was here that the performances of the review "Past and Present" were to be staged. And, although her husband was more interested in the operatic side of her career, he was uninhibitedly proud of the fact that she had almost literally sprung into fame in a night in the brilliant review for which his brother had written the music.

"It's a pity Oliver himself couldn't have been here," Anna heard Marcus Bannister say to Teresa. "But he's in New York of course for the Broadway production of the show. I've promised to hold a sort of watching brief for him, however."

"Then you must come down to the Tithe Barn also and meet some of our other performers," Teresa replied. "They'll be thrilled to have either of the famous Bannister brothers among them. Are you coming too, Mother?"

Mrs. Delawney said that she most certainly was. And they all went off together, leaving Anna to get on with her work in what was rather welcome isolation, except for the frequent ringing of the telephone.

It was more than halfway through the morning when, at the insistent summons of the phone bell, she lifted the receiver yet again and heard Jonathan Keyne's unmistakable voice ask,

"Is that you, Teresa?"

"No," she replied coolly. "Teresa is down at the Tithe

Barn. Can I do anything for you? This is Anna."

"Anna! I'm so glad to get you yourself. That's really why I rang up. I wanted you to know how desperately sorry I was not to be able to stay last night. But I simply had no choice."

"Oh, that's all right." She was pleased to hear how casually she managed to say that.

"I hope someone found time to explain the exact circumstances to you?"

"Yes, Teresa did. And then Rod added a few details."

"Then you do understand?" As she seemed to feel that called for no further confirmation, he went on after the slightest pause, "How did it go, Anna?"

"Very well, I think. Everyone seemed pleased. Marcus Bannister and his wife, Gail Rostall, came. He congratulated my father very warmly on the work, and Gail was a pupil of my teacher Elsa Marburger, so we had a lot to talk about together."

"I'm so glad. But, in spite of the interesting company, I hope I was a little bit missed."

"By whom?" The cool tone was a few degrees cooler.

"By you, of course. You were going to sing specially for me – remember?"

"Yes, I remember."

"Anna, you *haven't* forgiven me. I can hear it in your voice. I tell you – I'm more sorry than I can say – "

"Then why bother to say it?" she asked with unbelievable dryness. "And I do understand quite well. There are times when an urgent phone call can make other things seem quite unimportant. Like the time I heard about my mother being so ill."

"Is *that* the trouble? Is that what you're holding against me? All right, then, I was not as understanding and sympathetic as I should have been on that occasion, and

I'm damned sorry about it. This wasn't a parallel case, exactly, but – "

"No, it wasn't, was it? But really, it isn't worth all this discussion." Anna's brisk tone suggested that she was the busy secretary wanting to get on with something that was really important. "You were coming to the rehearsal, but you didn't make it after all. So what? There were enough people there to make the vital decision, so that the church concert will be held and the song cycle included. It's to be on the Tuesday of the second week. I expect you'll be here to hear it then, but if not – "

"Of course I'll be there!" he interrupted violently. "You talk as though it's of no interest to me, whereas you know perfectly well that it's the most important thing in the Festival to me now."

"Well, it's nice of you to say so. But it was really Teresa you wanted to speak to, wasn't it? She'll be back in about an hour's time. Shall I get her to call you back?"

There was quite a pause. Then he said, in a tone as cool as her own, "Yes, please." And he rang off.

Well, she told herself, she had dealt with the situation admirably. She had really managed to sound as though she had hardly missed him last night. *That* would teach him.

But teach him what? – She was not at all sure. And, in spite of the fact that she felt she had come off the better in that encounter, she wiped away a couple of unexpected tears before going on with her work.

At lunchtime Anna was made to feel immediately the difference in her status, now that she had become an artist in the Festival rather than just someone who was helping out in the office. In other words, for the first time it was assumed that she would join the house party at lunch, though whether on the insistence of Mrs. Delawney or because the Bannisters quite obviously expected her to be there, she was not quite sure.

In any case, it was an interesting occasion, with much discussion about Gail's part in the review, and many questions about the rest of the Festival programme from Marcus Bannister.

"I gather that Warrender is interested and will probably be here?" he said to Teresa.

And Teresa was able to reply happily that both the Warrenders were expected for part of the Festival, though she was not at present sure exactly which events they would be attending.

"They will, like you, be staying here in the house, of course," she added.

"And without doubt they will include the church concert during the second week," her mother amplified. "It was Mr. Warrender himself, you know, who gave the provocative interview to the *Daily Echo* which riveted our interest and sent us all last night to hear Mr. Fulroyd's song cycle."

"Was it really?" Gail looked amused. "That isn't like him. He's usually rather disagreeable about newspaper interviews or items for gossip columns."

"Then it's all the more gratifying that he should have made an exception for us," declared Mrs. Delawney contentedly.

"Indeed yes. But I thought – " Marcus Bannister frowned slightly, as though trying to recall something – "I know Brian Eden, the chap on the *Echo* who wrote up that account of the Festival. It was he who first drew my attention to the work we heard last night. I thought he said he got his information direct from you, Miss Delawney."

"No." Teresa shook her head decidedly. "Not from me."

"Perhaps from your secretary, then," said Marcus, and he went on with his admirable lunch, entirely unaware that the secretary was sitting opposite him, since to him she was more properly one of the Festival artists.

No one said anything for a moment. Then Mrs. Delawney changed the subject, and Anna breathed again. Though cautiously.

After lunch she went back to her study, expecting that any moment the door would open to admit a suspicious Teresa in a questioning mood. When the door did finally open, however, it was Mrs. Delawney who came in, and what she said was:

"How very naughty of you, Anna. But rather ingenious too. And very fortunate, I suppose one must say. Because if you hadn't pumped all that stuff into the *Daily Echo* man we wouldn't now be having the church concert. But just why did Jonathan spring to your defence, and put it all on to Oscar Warrender?"

"I don't know." Anna felt unable – indeed, since she genuinely liked Mrs. Delawney, she was also unwilling – to elaborate her deception further. "I'm ashamed now to think what I did. But it was on the spur of the moment, and because I knew how much it would mean to my father, as well as to myself. You see, the *Daily Echo* phoned while I was on my own and asked for what they called an interesting story about the Festival. It – it seemed the last chance to get anything done. And it *was* true that Oscar Warrender had heard the work and thought it good and said it must be included in the Festival."

"Well, I suppose I would have done the same thing in your place," said Mrs. Delawney unexpectedly. "But I still don't understand why Jonathan reacted the way he did. Possibly he was so curious about the work that he was determined to hear it for himself at all costs. Such a pity that in the end he was prevented from coming last night."

"Yes, wasn't it?" agreed Anna in a small voice.

"Just one of those things that one can't argue with, unfortunately. Fancy the old man dying just at that moment. I would have said he was tough enough to last another twenty years."

"Was Jon – Was Mr. Keyne so devoted to him, then?" asked Anna, as she had asked Rod.

"No, I don't imagine so. Nathaniel Bretherton wasn't the sort of person to whom one would be personally devoted. It was the question of the money."

"The – money?" Anna simply could not keep a note of scorn and distaste from her voice. For to be left in the lurch for family devotion, however misplaced, was bad enough, but to be ditched on a vital occasion for *money* was simply not to be borne.

"No need to use that tone, my dear," said Mrs. Delawney reprovingly. "Money can be very important – as well as unimportant. In this case, the whole financing of Jonathan's Canadian tour depended on it, you must remember. Which meant that he was committed on behalf of a good many other people too."

"You mean that he was just relying on the death of his grandfather at the right moment in order to finance his tour!"

"No, of course not." Mrs. Delawney laughed. "I forgot that you don't know as much about the family as we do. Old Nat Bretherton must be worth – oh, I don't know – but a very tidy fortune indeed. Like most men who make a great deal of money, he could be very nasty about it –"

She paused for a moment's reflection, and Anna wondered if she were mentally including her own husband under this general stricture or allowing him the status of an honourable exception.

"There were only two members of the family who might inherit," Mrs. Delawney went on after a moment. "Jonathan and a rather unlikeable cousin called, of all things, Saul. (Why *do* people christen their defenceless children by these ridiculous biblical names? It starts them off on the wrong foot right away.) Anyway, the old man felt it gave him a sense of power, I suppose, to dangle the prospect of a rich inheritance before first one grandson and then the other. Saul responded with gratifying anxiety, but Jonathan with maddening indifference. Then came this chance for him to do a Canadian opera tour. It's to be some time in the spring of next year – "

"I know," said Anna, biting her lip.

"Well, what Jonathan needed then, of course, was capital – and at once. So he boldly asked the old man for a pretty large lump sum, on the understanding that Saul should have everything else when it came to inheriting."

"Wasn't that rather short-sighted of him?"

"In some ways – yes. He stood to lose a great deal. On the other hand, Jonathan isn't the sort of man to stand about waiting for dead men's shoes. He saw this as his great artistic chance, from which he could begin to carve out an honourable career for himself. He needed support *then*. To most artists, money at the right time is usually the first vital step to a great career. Provided there is real talent there too, of course."

"So, if we pursue biblical parallels – " Anna smiled slightly – "he sold his birthright for a mess of potage?"

"Well, it was a pretty handsome mess of potage, I don't doubt," Mrs. Delawney laughed. "You don't finance an opera tour on less than a lot of money. Anyway, the old man agreed, rather pleased, I'm afraid, to have discovered something so important to Jonathan that he could put pressure on him. Having changed his will in favour of Saul, he tried to make his more independent grandson sit up and beg for the promised amount."

"He must have been an odious old man!" exclaimed Anna. "Even if one shouldn't speak ill of the dead," she added belatedly.

"Certainly one should speak ill of the dead if they deserve it," retorted Mrs. Delawney briskly. "Dying is not, in my view, an act which secures one immunity from criticism. After all, it is usually a purely involuntary action, and I'm certain it was in Nat Bretherton's case."

"Anyway, what happened?" asked Anna anxiously.

"Having accepted the idea of cutting Jonathan out of his will, the old man began to dither about handing over the sum he had promised. I suppose he enjoyed putting Jonathan through the hoops. But, anxious though he must have been, I don't think Jonathan gave much satisfaction. He's a proud man, and was determined not to show anxiety just to give pleasure to a mean old scoundrel. But he must have been through a pretty rough time lately. And then the old man died – and no one knows if he had completed the transfer of the money to Jonathan or not."

"Then you mean – " Anna was wide-eyed with horror – "that all Jonathan's hopes and plans for the Canadian tour may be smashed, after all?"

"Of course. Along with the hopes and plans of the friends and colleagues to whom he had made commitments. No wonder the poor fellow went rushing up to London to find out the truth."

"Oh, how awful for him! – how awful. I just didn't understand," exclaimed Anna remorsefully.

"Well, you couldn't very well, until someone explained

it to you," replied Mrs. Delawney practically. "It's a complicated position enough, heaven knows."

"But I meant – " But Anna could not say just what she meant, because she could think only of Jonathan saying that he hoped someone had explained the exact circumstances to her – and of her replying with indifferent airiness that they had, and so what?

After a moment she brought her attention back to Mrs. Delawney and asked almost fearfully,

"What will he *do*? If his grandfather hasn't transferred the money to him in time, I mean. Will he have to cancel the tour?"

"Of course. Unless – " Mrs. Delawney bit her lip thoughtfully. Then she gave a dry little smile. "Do you really want to know what I think?"

"If you feel like telling me – yes."

"I think he'll marry Teresa." She apparently didn't hear Anna catch her breath, for she went on calmly, "They like each other well enough. She's her father's favourite – " suddenly it was curiously obvious that she was not her mother's – "and I imagine any financial problem would be solved quite satisfactorily by my husband."

"Then you think – " again there was that touch of unhappy distaste in Anna's voice – "that Jonathan Keyne is the kind of man to marry for money?"

"That's the second time you've spoken loftily about money, which is silly of you," Mrs. Delawney told her realistically. "Money, properly spent, can do a lot of remarkable and admirable things. And plenty of reasonably nice people marry largely for money, even if they don't always admit it. I did myself, come to that," she added thoughtfully. "But at least I was frank about it."

"O-oh," said Anna, somewhat nonplussed, and she

could not help wondering if the frankness had extended to Mr. Delawney.

"Now, how did we come to be discussing *that*?" the older woman laughed suddenly. "I suppose mostly because you're a very good listener and a really nice girl. But understand, of course, that nothing which has been said should be repeated outside this room."

"That goes without saying!"

"And don't worry about Teresa's reactions to what Marcus Bannister let slip at lunchtime. I shall tell her that I had a talk with you and am convinced you had nothing to do with the giving of information to the *Daily Echo*."

"But, Mrs. Delawney, do you suppose she will be satisfied with that?"

"No, of course not. But when she questions you, you simply say you've been catechised enough already and you resent any further questions. Say it with that cool, off-putting little air of yours, and it will be difficult for her to take things further."

"*Have* I got a cool, off-putting air?" asked Anna, surprised.

"Certainly you have. I imagine that's what keeps Rod guessing." And with this last enigmatical remark Mrs. Delawney went out of the room.

Rod? – Oh, well, she couldn't bother about Rod at the moment. What mattered was that she had deeply misjudged Jonathan and added to his anxiety and unhappiness just when he needed support. And all about a trifle!

Incredibly enough, that was how his defection the previous evening seemed to her now. Just a trifle. Unavoidably, he had not been able to hear her sing then. But she could sing for him another time, surely? *Specially* for him, if that was how he cared to put it. She would have to apologise first, of course. She owed him that.

For a chill minute or so she wondered if he would be in any mood to listen to an apology. But she must somehow make an occasion. The important thing was that he should not have his hopes and plans shattered – and that he should know it was only a misunderstanding which had made her so coldly unsympathetic.

If she had known where to telephone him she would have called him then. But somehow Jonathan's private London number had never appeared on any list Teresa had given her. Teresa knew it, of course. But she could no more ask Teresa for that telephone number than she could ask her the amount of her bank balance.

Whatever Mrs. Delawney said to her daughter must have satisfied, or at least silenced, her. For she made no further reference to the *Daily Echo* feature, so far as Anna was concerned. Instead, she just threw herself with increased energy into the Festival arrangements, keenly aware – as they all were by now – that the first night was no more than ten days away.

The opening event, which was to be on a Saturday night, was the first performance of the Bannister-Mallender review, "Past and Present". It was to take place in the transformed Tithe Barn and be open to the general public. On Sunday there was to be a concert of chamber music at Coppershaw Grange for an invited audience, the concert itself to take place in the big drawing-room and be followed by a buffet party.

Anna found, a little to her surprise, that both she and her father were among the invited guests, and again she realised how their status had changed since they had become Festival artists. Even, in view of the excitement over the song cycle, important Festival artists.

She would have been less than human if she had not greatly enjoyed this transformation, and her pleasure was heightened by the delight of her mother, when she visited her at the convalescent home and described in full the triumph of the Fulroyd family.

"Anna dear, what this must mean to your father!" exclaimed Mrs. Fulroyd, her face flushed and her eyes shining with family pride and joy.

"I know. He's like a different person," Anna agreed. "And I'm so happy too, of course," she added.

"Really happy?" asked her mother unexpectedly.

"Of course! What makes you ask?"

"There's a sort of gravity – anxiety – about you. Oh, I know you've been anxious about me. But that's over now and you know it. I wondered – " she paused and then said – "I'm not trying to force any confidences. I just wondered if you'd been – disappointed in someone who mattered rather a lot."

"Mother, you're a witch!" Anna gave a half vexed little laugh. "I was disappointed, temporarily. You see, the most important – and most interesting – man in the Festival was supposed to come specially to hear me, the evening they all came from the Grange to hear the song cycle. He told me he was coming specially and – and asked me to sing for *him*."

"Was he personally important to you, do you mean?"

"Y-yes," said Anna, reluctant to make the admission to anyone, yet strangely moved and excited to be putting the fact into words.

"And what happened?"

"At the last minute he didn't come. He sent an excuse which sounded – paltry. And I was so angry that when he telephoned next day I let him *know* I was angry. Then I found out afterwards that he had every reason to be missing; he had been called to London on a matter that was absolutely vital to him and his career. I can't help – worrying a little until I can put things right."

"But can't you just telephone him and say there was a misunderstanding and that you want to apologise and put things right?"

"I haven't got his phone number," said Anna slowly.

"Haven't got his phone number?" Her mother sounded astonished. "I thought you were implying that you knew him quite well."

"Oh, I do – I do. In a way. But there are complications." She sighed, and then saw she must say more since she had got so far. "Teresa Delawney is keen on him too," she said, and only when she saw her mother's eyebrows rise did she realise that she had let slip that revealing word "too". She coloured and went on quickly, "Perhaps I should say that Teresa is the possessive kind and wouldn't like it if she thought – if she thought he and I were specially friendly."

"And are you specially friendly?"

"Mother, I don't *know*! I mean I don't know how he feels."

"Do you know how you feel?" asked her mother practically. And for a whole minute Anna was silent, looking down at her hands which were clasped in her lap.

Then she said slowly, "I like him – a lot. It could be more than that. But I dare not let it be in case – in case he chooses Teresa."

"You think he's really fonder of her?"

"No, I don't!" cried Anna with sudden angry conviction.

Her mother looked at her consideringly and said in a matter-of-fact tone, "Then I don't really see your problem."

"No, I realise I'm not making this very clear." Anna ruffled up her hair distractedly. "Mother, he's a professional musician. Quite a brilliant conductor in his own right, but even more a director and organiser of near-genius. The kind of man who, given his chance, might become one of the great operatic directors, and there are few enough of them, heaven knows."

"I take it this is the man who wants you to go on an opera tour next year?"

"Go on – ? Oh, yes. Yes, of course," agreed Anna, suddenly remembering the mixture of fact and fiction with which she had reassured her mother about her leaving her London studies for so long. "It would be a Canadian tour in exceptionally good circumstances. The kind of thing which would mean a tremendous step forward in his career. The financing of it was all apparently secure. But now something disastrous has happened. It's possible that the finance won't be forthcoming after all. If he doesn't want a fearful setback, he *must* find backing elsewhere."

She paused so long that her mother said, "I'm following you."

"If he married Teresa – and that's what she wants – the Delawney fortune would be more or less behind him."

"And you think that would be too strong a temptation for him to resist?"

"I don't know, Mother – I don't know." Anna spread out her hands in a gesture of helplessness. "If things aren't as bad as he – as all of us fear, then he would be independent of anything the Delawneys could or would do for him. But if not – well, there aren't many fortunes like the Delawneys', and he might feel it was – unrealistic to ignore that fact."

"Yours isn't a very well-based romance, then, is it?"

Her mother, with her natural inclination to face facts, spoke frankly.

"No," said Anna, though she winced a little. "That's why I tell myself that – that there's probably nothing in it for me."

"Well, I'm sorry, my dear. But I think you're being wise."

"I think so too," replied Anna, under the momentary impression that she was somehow coming to a vital conclusion during this talk with her mother.

But during her long bus journey home she knew she was not being wise at all. She stared out of the window and thought of Jonathan kissing her, and how the world had changed because of it, and later she had sung as she had never sung before. It had been her innocent paean of triumph because for that very short time she believed he loved her.

As the bus stopped right outside the Tithe Barn, and she could see, from the lights and the signs of general activity, that a rehearsal was still in progress, she got off and went in. There were quite a number of people connected with the company standing or sitting about in the improvised auditorium, and she slipped into a seat beside Mrs. Delawney in one of the back rows.

"Has the rehearsal gone well?" she asked in a discreet undertone.

"Very well indeed," replied Mrs. Delawney in the same tone. "Gail Rostall really is a gifted creature, and it's quite touching to see how willingly she and Marcus help the non-professionals. How did you find your mother?"

"Making excellent progress. She won't be strong enough to come to any of the performances, I'm afraid. But she greatly enjoyed hearing about all that has been happening."

"Good." Mrs. Delawney spoke absently and then turned as there was a slight stir near the door and one or two other people came in. Anna turned too and saw, with a slight shock of excitement which set her heart thumping, that Jonathan was among them.

She heard her companion give an exclamation, and she got up and went to him, while Anna, hardly knowing what she was doing, got up also and followed her, slowly but as though she could not help herself.

She came up just in time to hear Mrs. Delawney say, "I'm not going to beat about the bush, Jonathan. How have things worked out?"

"Very well for Saul." He looked tired and strained, but he managed a wry little smile. "The old man had signed nothing so far as I'm concerned. Saul takes the lot."

CHAPTER SEVEN

"Your cousin inherits everything?" Mrs. Delawney looked at Jonathan in consternation. "You mean you get nothing at all under your grandfather's will?"

"That was the agreed arrangement, you remember." Jonathan suddenly sounded as weary and dispirited as he looked. "My share was to come to me during the old man's lifetime. He didn't live long enough to complete the transaction, that's all."

"But surely – won't Saul feel he has some sort of moral obligation towards you?"

"No. He isn't very hot on moral obligations. We met and discussed things, of course. But he stands by the actual wording of the recent will, which states that everything of which Nathaniel Bretherton dies possessed goes to his grandson Saul. Let's not bother to talk about it. I think someone over by the stage is trying to attract your attention."

"Where?" Mrs. Delawney glanced over her shoulder. "Oh – " she turned and left him. And suddenly Anna knew that this was her moment.

"Jonathan" – she took his hand and was surprised to find it rather cold – "I know what I'm going to say can't be very important compared with what has happened to you in the last few days. But I just want to tell you how truly sorry I am that I was so horrid to you on the phone. It was a mistake. I thought – "

"Were you horrid to me on the phone?" He smiled faintly, and returned her handclasp with unexpected warmth.

"Of course. You tried to apologise for not turning up to hear the try-out of my father's song cycle. And I brushed you off and pretended it didn't matter to me whether you were there or not."

"And did it matter?"

"Yes. A lot," she said simply.

"I'm sorry, my dear. I really couldn't help myself."

"Oh, it doesn't matter *now*! Not now that I know you had every reason not to be there. You said on the phone that you hoped someone had explained the circumstances to me and I said they had. But they hadn't. It wasn't until later that I heard about the significance of your grandfather's death. It must have seemed that I was taking offence in the most ridiculous and unsympathetic way, just when you needed the support of – of your friends. I'm so very sorry. Please forgive me."

"There's nothing to forgive." For a moment he touched her cheek with the back of his fingers, in that light caress he had used once before. "Come and sit with me, Anna, and let's hear Gail do the Spanish number. It looks to me as though she's just about to do it."

And, taking Anna's hand in his again, he led the way to a couple of side seats, and there they sat, their hands still lightly intertwined, and listened to the song from "Past and Present" which had contributed so signally to the first night success of that now famous review.

Anna had never actually heard it before, and she listened in delight to the gay, provocative tune which Gail sang first as a girl who was trying unashamedly to attract every man who passed – and succeeding. Then someone who was obviously the only man who mattered to her came strolling past, giving her no more than one glance of contemptuous rejection. The girl on the stage stood staring after him for a moment, and then turned and went slowly in the opposite direction. As she did so, she sang her haunting tune again. But this time it was neither gay nor provocative. It had somehow become a sad little lament for everyone's lost dreams.

"It gets me every time she does it," declared Jonathan, his appreciation of Gail Rostall's art having apparently made him almost forget his own problems.

"I've never heard her do it before. She's wonderful!"

"People remember it long after they've forgotten all the things in the show that have made them laugh. It's a stroke of genius. And, talking of genius, Warrender tells me that I have a real experience in store when I finally hear your father's song cycle. I told him, by the way, about the *Daily Echo* incident."

"Was he annoyed?" asked Anna rather apprehensively.

"No, I think he was a good deal amused. Anyway, he agreed to accept responsibility for having leaked information to the Press, so your criminal tracks have been safely covered."

"They were very nearly completely *un*covered by an innocent remark from Marcus Bannister at lunch some days ago," Anna told him ruefully. "Not that it matters now, of course. But Mrs. Delawney guessed the truth at that point."

"She did?" Jonathan sounded amused, and he added with something like a note of affection in his voice, "She's pretty smart, Mrs. Delawney."

And then Teresa came across the hall and he unobtrusively released Anna's hand and stood up.

"I'm sorry, my dear! Mother's just told me — " Teresa took him by the arm and they moved away, their heads close together in friendly, intimate conversation.

Anna went on sitting where she was for a while, telling herself that she hardly minded his going. She had had *her* wonderful few minutes, and there was no misunderstanding between them any more. All the same –

"And how is my favourite festival artist?" enquired Roderick Delawney's pleasant, gay voice behind her. "I looked for you most of the afternoon but couldn't find you."

"I went to visit my mother in the convalescent home." She turned to smile at him with genuine pleasure. "It's a long bus journey, you know, and takes quite a while."

"Why didn't you ask me to drive you through? I'd be happy to take you any time I'm home."

"Oh, I couldn't possibly let you hang about all the afternoon while I was visiting Mother! I don't really mind the bus journey. But I am a bit tired now and I think I'd better go home."

"Well, at least I'll drive you home," he insisted.

She thanked him, trying not to commit the unforgivable sin of looking round for one person while she was talking to another. Then she caught sight of Jonathan. But he was still with Teresa, and they were talking to the Bannisters now, so without making a determined interruption she could hardly say good-night to him.

She went out into the night with Rod instead, feeling more than a little frustrated. But, if she could not talk any more *to* Jonathan, she could at least allow herself the luxury of talking *of* him. And she said, as they drove away from the Tithe Barn,

"Did you hear that Jonathan Keyne is not going to get the money due to him from his grandfather?"

"I never thought he would," retorted Rod cheerfully. "Nat Bretherton was determined not to let him have it. He was a mean old cuss and always resented Jonathan's independent air towards him and his fortune. He was determined to have the last word – if only from beyond the grave, as the saying is."

"I think it was disgusting of him!" Anna's voice trembled with the intensity of her indignation.

"Well, of course it was. But that's the sort of thing his type does," replied Rod philosophically. "Jonathan will find a way out of the mess somehow."

"But *how*? He either has the money to back his opera tour or he hasn't."

"Money isn't all that difficult to come by, if you know where to look for it," declared Rod, with all the easy assurance of someone who has never had to worry about what tomorrow may bring.

"Of course it is! A huge sum like that, I mean. It costs — oh, I don't know how much — to finance an opera tour. Even a modest one."

"You don't get it all from one source, Anna. Unless you're dealing with someone as disgustingly rich as old Nat Bretherton. Or my father."

The mention of his father silenced her, and it was a few moments before she could bring herself to ask, with desperate casualness, "Do you think your father would be prepared to help?"

"Only if he had some compelling reason for doing so. He's let Teresa have a packet for this festival. She — or anyone else — would have to put up a very good case before he would give any more in support of the arts. Which are, incidentally, a closed book to him anyway, so why should he bother?"

"Then, you see, it *isn't* so easy to get the money as you said at first," she exclaimed almost irritably.

"There are other people besides my father."

"Who, for instance?" she challenged him.

"Myself, for one," he replied lightly.

"You, Rod?" She turned and stared at him. "But are

you as rich as that?" she asked naively.

"Not all on my own." He laughed. "But I always know where to put my hand on money in a big way. These things are largely a matter of book-keeping, you know," he explained carelessly. "Firms and individuals set off one thing against another. And there are those who will do something for the arts, either for kudos or even profit."

"And you really know that sort of person?" a very faint, excited hope began to stir in her.

"If I looked hard enough, I don't doubt I could find them."

"And *would* you do that for Jonathan, Rod?"

"I might. If there were someone in his company whose future interested me sufficiently, for instance." He gave her a sidelong glance, but she was too deedly absorbed in her own thoughts to notice.

"You mean – other than Jonathan himself?"

"Oh, yes, other than Jonathan himself. I have quite a high regard for him, but I woudln't go to all that trouble and risk just for his blue eyes."

And suddenly she had not the courage to ask for whose blue eyes he *would* do it. She just fell into a long and thoughtful silence for the rest of the short journey. And presently, when they arrived, Rod kissed her before she got out of the car, as though that had somehow become the natural way for him to take leave of her.

She tried not to think just what that conversation had implied. At first, the idea that he might possibly know how to come to Jonathan's rescue had been so exciting that it remained the only consideration in her mind. But there was no mistaking where *his* line of reasoning led after that.

There had been nothing unpleasant or suggestive about

his way of putting it. On the contrary, it had been an almost tactful way of letting her know that here was someone who might interest himself in her career, to the extent of helping to back some enterprise if she were in it.

If he had been an elderly patron of the arts in his own right, the position would have been much less tricky. But he was not. Far from it. He cheerfully declared himself to be something of a philistine, and he was, by any girl's standards, an attractive young man.

"I can't think about it just now!" Anna told herself desperately. "It's too complicated. Besides, Jonathan himself may manage to find supporters. Other than – than Mr. Delawney, I mean. For the time being I must concentrate on my part in the Festival. Otherwise I shan't do well, and then everyone will be disappointed and Dad's triumph will be ruined. But how soon must Jonathan make a decision either to cancel or go ahead? How much time is left?"

This sensation of planning against time took on an extra sense of urgency now since the last days of preparation for the Festival were slipping away, and everyone seemed to be concerned with some deadline or other.

Then, all at once, it was the first night, and they were all gathering in the Tithe Barn for the opening performance of "Past and Present". And from the very beginning the sweet scent of success was in the air.

The local performers were very good indeed. And the one or two imported "stars", like Gail Rostall, were integrated into the company so skilfully that they gave an air of great distinction without drawing an embarrassingly sharp line between professional and semi-amateur.

The audience loved it all, and at the end there was a genuine ovation. Not only for the players, but for Teresa too. For without her, as everyone well knew, there would not have been a Festival.

She was looking lovely. Anna admitted the fact to herself wholeheartedly, as she studied the deceptively simple black dress which somehow made Teresa look much the most distinguished woman there. She said a few charming words from the stage, paying warm tribute to the help she had received from "my good friend, Jonathan Keyne". Then he joined her, and they stood there, laughing happily and holding hands while everyone said what a delightful pair they made.

No one mentioned how signally Mr. Delawney's cold cash had contributed to the success of the venture. But he sat in the front row, his glance resting so indulgently upon his daughter that Anna found herself thinking, "He wouldn't hesitate to back Jonathan to the hilt if Teresa said that was what she wanted most in the world."

She tried not to feel mean-spirited or jealous. But her heart ached almost physically, and she found some difficulty in giving the impression that she too was light-heartedly enjoying this great occasion.

That successful first night set the tone for the whole Festival. It was as though they could do no wrong, and public and critics combined to praise almost every event. While the more private occasions, which took place in Coppershaw Grange itself, attained such a height of social and artistic prestige that invitations to them were coveted by all and sundry.

However little she might like Teresa, however bitterly it hurt to see her and Jonathan constantly together, Anna could not in all justice withhold her deepest admiration for her vision and efficiency. And if *she* could feel like that, how must Jonathan view this clever, attractive girl, who made little secret of her preference for him?

Not until the end of the first week was there the slightest slackening of interest and happy tension. Then, as Teresa had herself predicted, people became almost used to enjoying themselves and began to look for something quite out of the ordinary to quicken their enthusiasm once more. And this was the point at which Teresa began to let everything centre round the attraction of the church concert, with the song cycle as its highlight.

Hints and promises were dropped here and there in the Press and among her own immediate circle. She let it be known that only now had the famous Warrenders come to see what the Festival could offer – sure indication that they were expecting something very special. Local pride and curiosity were stimulated to a quite astonishing degree, and Anna suddenly found herself a figure of interest to an extent she had scarcely anticipated.

She knew, of course, that it was not for any love of herself that Teresa was doing all this. It was merely that she had now become a valuable factor in Teresa's whole project, and as such she must be "promoted" in the most effective way.

To her surprise, she received letters and telegrams of good wishes from quite a number of people, including some of her fellow students in London who had presumably read the advance publicity about her. But what moved and delighted her most was a box of exquisite roses from Jonathan, enclosing a card on which he had written:

"Forgive me for that other time and sing for me tonight instead. Love – Jonathan."

Oh, she knew people in the theatrical and musical world used the word "love" when they didn't necessarily mean anything of the kind. But just to see the word, followed by his name, excited and thrilled her, so that she could hardly wait for the moment when she was to sing specially for him, and justify all the hopes and plans which had gone into the arranging of this night.

As she walked with her father the short distance to the church, she was heartwarmingly aware that she was still the girl in her own home town, however much had been done to make her into something of a star for this occasion. For several people waved to her and called out greetings and good wishes as she passed.

She had never seen the church so full, nor so many unknown faces. And right there in the front, with his beautiful wife Anthea, was Oscar Warrender – with a faint smile and a gracious inclination of his head for her father. Beside them, clear for her to see this time, was Jonathan.

She had thought at that famous rehearsal that neither she nor the choir could ever do any better than they had then. But there is a subtle atmosphere about a really great occasion which sets a sort of electric current coursing between audience and performers, raising everything to a peak of perfection beyond the most optimistic expectations.

It is impossible to describe and equally impossible to ignore, and no one has ever been able to explain it entirely. Does the splendour of the performance raise the interest and sympathy of the audience to fever pitch? or does the audience's instinctive awareness that this is a unique occasion communicate itself to the performers and enable them to give better than their best?

Whichever it was on this occasion, Anna knew from the moment she stood up that this was to be one of the great performances of her life. That Jonathan was there in front of her had something to do with it, of course – but not all. That the great Oscar Warrender had expressed his belief in her and her father also played its part. But, over and above those two things, she drew on something within herself. That power to transport people, which Judy had spoken of long ago.

On that evening she knew for a certainty that she crossed the almost unbridgeable gap which lies between the admirable performer and the artist with a touch of greatness.

It is still a moot point whether a church audience should applaud or not, though for a non-religious work it is usually regarded as permissible. That night there was no question about it. The reception of the song cycle was sensational, and it was difficult to say for whom was the greater share, Anna or her father. The choir also stood for their well-earned applause, Tommy Bream even inclining his head from time to time in what, Anna greatly feared, was a splendid "take-off" of Oscar Warrender's rather lordly bow.

It was over at last, and people were pouring out of the church, though many lingered outside to exchange comments and shower fresh praise on the artists as they came out. Anna was surrounded by old friends and neighbours, many of whom said warmly how happy her mother would be. And for quite a while she lost sight of the party from Coppershaw Grange.

All who had taken part in the concert – including the choir, right down to Tommy Bream himself – had been invited back to the Grange for supper, and there was a great sorting out of cars and scrambling for places in the coach which was to take the choir members. In the flurry, Anna lost sight of even her father. Then he surfaced again beside her and said in a high, excited voice,

"We are to go with the Warrenders, I understand."

"No, no – you're coming with me." Jonathan's hand closed firmly round her arm. "It's all right, Mr. Fulroyd,

I'm taking Anna. We'll see you at the Grange."

And she was guided across the road and installed in Jonathan's car without more ado. Then, as he steered clear of the press of cars, she said, between eagerness and nervousness, "You haven't told me yet what you thought of it."

"I'll tell you properly when we get away from this mob," was the reply. And she leaned back again, content to wait, as she realised that he was not taking the short, straight run to the Grange, but was making the same detour he had made that first day when he had fetched her from home.

They were alone at last. Free of all the other cars, on a rising edge of moorland above the town. And here he stopped the car and turned to look at her.

She withstood his glance pretty well, though she was trembling a little. Then he bent forward and kissed her deliberately and said, "You wonderful, darling girl. Did you know that we all heard a miracle tonight?"

"Well, n-no. That's putting it a bit high, isn't it?" She laughed rather uncertainly.

But he didn't laugh. He leaned back with his arms folded and regarded her as a man might regard a great work of art that he was seeing for the first time.

"It happens only half a dozen times in the lifetime of even the luckiest of us," he said slowly. "To be there when a great talent suddenly flowers in all its complete perfection. Weren't you aware of it yourself?"

"I did know that something – flowered, as you say. Something that I've been working for for years just – happened. I don't know how else to describe it."

"The description will do." He put out his hand and passed it gently over her shining hair, as though he were touching something infinitely precious. "My dear – my very dear Anna, how does one say 'thank you' for such an experience?"

"I – I'm glad if you were so pleased with me," she stammered.

"*Pleased*!" He caught both her hands and held them close against him, so that she was drawn close to him also. "I haven't felt so thrilled and elated for years. I'm mad about – this voice of yours. I can't hear enough of it. I must have been insane ever to think I could bear to do the Canadian tour without you there. All right, you brushed me off once and I displayed a bit of angry pride. But who cares about that now? We *have* to work together, do you hear? You must be in my company – you simply must!"

"But is there going to *be* a company?" Her voice quivered with mingled hope and fear. "I thought it was a write-off after your grandfather – "

"Oh, to hell with that!" declared Jonathan. "It was a blow at the time. But what is one worth if one can't face a setback or two? Maybe it wouldn't have been good for me to have it all so easily. Sometimes one has to learn the hard way."

"Oh, Jonathan!" She knew in that moment that she loved him. "You really think you might bring it off, after all?"

"Yes," he nodded. "I might not be able to make it a spring tour. Perhaps there must be a postponement while I make fresh arrangements. But you'll wait, won't you, Anna? You'll wait and come with me when I've got things fixed. I couldn't bear to let anyone else have the handling of that talent."

"Yes, I'll wait." She felt dazed, as though she had been hit on the head by a shower of gold. "Yes, I'll – come with you."

"It's a bargain?" He took her face between his hands.

"Yes," she said breathlessly. "It's a bargain."

"That seals it, then." And he gave her a long kiss on her lips.

After that they drove on, with hardly another word between them. All the words which mattered had been said. And Anna who, earlier in the evening, had thought that perhaps she was the happiest girl in the country, knew now that she was the happiest girl in the world.

As they drove up to Coppershaw Grange, there were other cars still arriving and, as they joined the throng of people entering the house, Anna hoped no one would notice that she and Jonathan had taken rather longer over their journey than was strictly necessary.

Only one person noticed. At least, only one person remarked on it. And that was Teresa, who was standing in the hall, making everyone welcome. She smiled at them certainly, but Anna thought her eyes were cold and strangely anxious as they came up to her. Her tone, however, was quite gay as she asked,

"Where have you two been? I thought you were among the first to leave."

"I've been persuading Anna that she must work with me," replied Jonathan coolly. "She is going to join my company when I do the Canadian tour."

"The – ? But is there going to *be* a Canadian tour?" asked Teresa, in much the same words that Anna had used. "I thought it was very much in the balance."

"Oh, I think we'll manage somehow. I'm not so easily put off as my grandfather no doubt hoped," returned Jonathan with a smile, and he made to go on with Anna into the big drawing-room.

But Teresa caught him by the arm and said something in a low, urgent voice, which was so obviously meant for him alone that Anna felt bound to go on without him, much though she would have liked to know what was said.

It hardly mattered now, though, she realised suddenly. Teresa's exclamation alone had been enough to show that she and her father were not going to be responsible for financing any Canadian tour. Jonathan was not to be tied to her in any way. He was going to be independent – free to engage whatever artist he chose, free to like – or love – any girl, without owing any obligation to Teresa Delawney.

If it had been possible for her spirits to rise even higher, this reflection would have made her even more radiant. As it was, when she entered the drawing-room there was a little spattter of applause, and someone laughed and said,

"It's not difficult to see who is the queen of song this evening."

It was a woman's voice, and when Anna turned to see who had spoken, she saw it was Anthea Warrender, who smilingly raised her glass and drank to her.

Such a tribute from such a famous singer herself made Anna catch her breath, and she crossed the room to thank her.

"It's completely deserved, my dear," Anthea told her. "Tonight was a very great night for all of us."

"Oh, thank you!" Anna smiled shyly, and then instinctively glanced at the tall man who was standing beside Anthea.

"Yes," he confirmed, "you'll do. Provided you work hard, of course. Don't let tonight's triumph go to your head. You have a long way to go yet before you become an experienced, worthwhile artist. But the material is there, which is the first and absolute essential. What you do with it is the real test of you as a person and an artist."

"I know," Anna said earnestly. "I know. And I will work hard, I promise you."

"With whom?" enquired Warrender, a little sardonically. "That's important too, you know. When the news of this evening gets around you may well have several offers – most of them unsuitable at this present stage of your development. You had better ask me – or Jonathan – before you make any final decisions."

"Thank you, I will! And thank you also, Mr. Warrender, for all your kindness to my father."

"It was not kindness. It was a well-trained capacity for recognising talent in an unlikely place," retorted the conductor drily.

"Oh, Oscar! It was probably a dash of kindness too," protested Anthea amusedly. "You are rather nice sometimes, you know."

"My father described you that first evening as a dear, good man," Anna said, smiling. "I thought it rather incongruous at the time, to tell the truth. But I don't now. It's entirely thanks to you that he looks happier tonight than I've ever seen him look in all the years I've known him."

"I am overwhelmed," said Warrender, looking nothing of the kind, but he smiled not unkindly. "Your father is a greatly gifted musician, Miss Anna, but without much practical judgment. Possibly the natural stream of inspiration has remained all the clearer for that. But he needs a touch of worldly guidance."

It was pretty obvious who intended to supply the touch of worldly guidance, and Anna smiled gratefully at the famous conductor, before she turned to Rod Delawney who was waiting eagerly to add his share of congratulation to all that had gone before.

But, being a practical man, he also steered her firmly past all other admirers and led her to a splendid buffet declaring that she at least had sung for her supper and should be allowed to enjoy it now. Anna indeed found that she was extremely hungry after all the excitement and was only too glad to be installed in a fairly secluded corner, with an appetising selection of food and a glass of Mr. Delawney's best champagne.

"Though I suppose the excitement and congratulation is more heady than anything that ever came out of a bottle," Rod said, as he stood smiling down at her.

"The champagne is good too, Rod. *Everything* is wonderful!" Anna declared. "This is the greatest night of my life."

"So far," he amended. "I venture to prophesy there will be many, many triumphs still to come."

"You think so?" Smilingly she watched the bubbles rising in her glass. "Well, I'm daring to hope so too." And she thought of Jonathan and the Canadian tour, and suddenly it occurred to her that perhaps she should tell Rod about that. He was too nice to be allowed to go on thinking he might play a generous hand in her career when in fact there was no question of that.

"Rod, there's something else which makes tonight the most exciting thing ever," she said impulsively. "Jonathan is pretty sure that he *is* going to get the backing for that Canadian tour. And he wants me to be in the company."

"Yes, I know." He smiled down at her indulgently.

"You – know? But how do you know?" She glanced down at the champagne again lest the sudden bleak dismay which gripped her should show in her eyes.

"I had a word with him this evening. I told him that if you were in his company I'd see that he got his backing all right."

CHAPTER EIGHT

Suddenly there was a sharp, snapping sound, and Anna exclaimed, "Oh! I've broken my glass."

"Careful! Don't cut yourself." Rod was taking the two pieces from her. "The stem must have been cracked. I'll get you another glass."

"No – " she wiped a few cold drops of wine from her hand, with the strange impression that they had chilled her to the heart. "I don't want any more, thank you."

"Of course you do!" Rod would take no denial. And as he went from her, she looked after him and thought,

"So *that* was why Jonathan made such a fuss of me in the car and insisted that I must join his Canadian tour." The moving words, the unforgettable kiss, those magic moments of pure happiness, had all had a purpose.

"You must be in my company," he had said. "You simply must." And how right he was! She was a financial necessity for him. Well worth some romantic love-making.

She knew that possibly she was being unfair to him. His admiration for her voice and talent had been genuine enough. She had no need to doubt that. But what made her an irresistible asset to his company was the fact that Rod Delawney's powerful backing was dependent on her being a member.

"Oh, why did Rod have to tell me?" she thought wretchedly. "Now I shall never know how much was self-interest and how much real feeling. I'd still be happy if Rod hadn't spoken."

She was too much her mother's daughter to want anything but the stark truth, in the usual way. But in that moment she would gladly have remained in happy ignorance, rather than have her glorious illusions snatched from her. She looked round for Jonathan, as though the mere sight of him might help her to regain her confidence in him. But he was talking to Teresa and Mrs. Delawney, and seemed very cheerfully occupied.

Then she saw her father coming towards her, accompanied by Oscar Warrender, and she had to force a smile to her face and try to look once more as though this evening held nothing but joy for her.

"Anna dear, Mr. Warrender has been talking to me about your future." Her father's face at any rate was still alight with the happiness of contented achievement. "He feels very strongly that you should be in the hands of a really good manager or agent. His own manager – "

"Dermot Deane!" exclaimed Anna, recalling without effort the name of the most successful manager in London.

"Exactly." Warrender took over the conversation then. "He would have to hear you, of course, for himself. He couldn't be expected to take you on hearsay only, even on my recommendation. So I think you should come to London as soon as possible. There may be some very speedy reactions after tonight. And there are one or two useful people you should meet."

"To London? I don't know – " She turned quickly to her father. "Could you manage without me? Mother might be coming home almost any time now and – "

"Of course we can manage!" Never before had she seen her father so confident that he could cope with whatever happened. "Mrs. Ford would come in every day, and I'm not entirely helpless. In any case, enough time has been wasted already. This isn't the moment to let a few domestic details stand in the way of a great opportunity."

"How soon can you come, Anna?" Warrender had been standing by with a slightly impatient air while these family details were discussed.

"Any time you suggest," asserted Mr. Fulroyd, without waiting for his daughter to reply.

"Next week, then," said Warrender. "The first half of next week. I'll arrange for Deane to hear you on Tuesday or Wednesday. I can't answer for him in advance, of course, but I don't doubt he will want to take you on. You would be fairly safe in his hands. And he would understand that I should wish to be consulted about any offer made to you."

"Mr. Warrender – " she spoke a little uncertainly – "I have had one tentative offer made to me already. Jonathan Keyne wants me for his Canadian tour."

"But I thought you said there wasn't going to be a tour," her father interrupted in surprise. "Wasn't there trouble about financing it?"

"It seems that he's more hopeful, after all," replied Anna, without much expression in her voice.

"Yes, he said something about it to me this evening," Oscar Warrender agreed carelessly. "Support from quite an unexpected quarter, I believe. Well, such a tour would provide you with excellent experience, of course. But we won't count on anything at this point. Where will you be staying in London?"

Anna gave him the address and telephone number of the flat she had shared during most of her student days, for she felt pretty confident that she could always have a bed there.

"I'll be there by Monday," she promised.

And as Warrender gave an approving nod and moved off with her father, she saw Jonathan coming towards her.

She stood up, trying to control a small nervous tremor, and said hastily, "I was looking for Rod Delawney."

"Were you?" His glance was suddenly amused. "He's a very ardent admirer of yours, isn't he?"

"He thinks I sing well – yes," she said confusedly.

"Don't we all?" retorted Jonathan with a laugh. "Had Warrender anything interesting to say to you?"

"Yes, indeed!" she seized eagerly on an unembarrassing topic. "He wants me to go to London next week and sing for Dermot Deane. He thinks I should try to get him to represent me."

"You couldn't do better. And with Warrender's recommendation there isn't much doubt about Deane's reaction. But, Anna – " he put his hand lightly round her arm – "don't let him talk you into anything that would clash with the Canadian tour."

With an effort, she forced a slight, protesting laugh.

"Oh, I'm not expecting fierce competition for my services at this stage. Perhaps no one else will want me for anything. And even you might have second thoughts, in certain circumstances."

"What nonsense! and in what circumstances, for heaven's sake?"

"Oh, one never knows." She gave a careless little shrug, which somehow removed his hand from her arm. "Here comes Rod, with my champagne."

She knew that Jonathan's glance was on her with a sort of puzzled disquiet. But she smiled determinedly at Rod as he apologised for having left her for so long, and pretended that all her attention was on him. After a moment she realised that Jonathan had moved away. Possibly, of course, he felt faintly uncomfortable in the company of Rod and herself together.

Soon after that there began to be a stir of departure.

The choir were making their good-byes and moving out to the waiting coach, and several of the other guests said they must go too.

"Rod, I'm suddenly dreadfully tired," Anna said. "Do you think you could drive Dad and me down home?"

"I was going to anyway," Rod assured her. "Shall I go and detach your father from Warrender? They seem to have become great buddies."

"I know. It's the most wonderful thing that ever happened to Dad." She smiled a little remorsefully. "It's a shame to cut his pleasure short."

But at that moment her father caught her glance and came over to say on his own account that he thought it was time they made a move. That made things easy for her. She only had to have a word with Teresa, thanking her for her hospitality, and also for the great chance which the evening's concert had meant for her.

"Don't thank *me*!" Teresa smiled with that touch of graciousness which did nothing to warm the heart. "The thanks are due to you and your father. I can't wait to see the reviews. Though I don't expect there will be anything in the London papers until Thursday. There wouldn't be time. Have a lazy time at home tomorrow. You've earned it."

It was a charming dismissal – but a dismissal. And then Anna was on the way out with Rod and her father. With relief or regret – she was not quite sure which – there was no need for more than a casual little wave of good-bye to Jonathan across the room.

He started forward, she saw. But somehow Teresa moved across his path, with a smiling word or two to him. And a moment later they were out of the room, and then out of the house and in Rod's car.

She managed that her father went in front with Rod.

And, by replying in no more than monosyllables to anything addressed to her, she contrived to give the impression that she was already half asleep. Even her good-night to Rod, though becomingly grateful and friendly, was brief. And the moment they were inside the house, her father said,

"Bed for you right away, my dear. I can see you're beginning to get the reaction after this astounding evening. What you need is a good night's sleep."

"You're right. It's all been wonderful, but I'm suddenly almost dead." Convincingly, she stifled another yawn, and her father laughed and kissed her good-night and watched her slowly mount the stairs apparently in the last stages of exhaustion.

But the moment she was alone in her room she tossed off her clothes and made ready for bed with a sort of desperate haste. She was alone! She was alone at last, with no need to pretend to anyone, and she sat down on the side of her bed and buried her face in her hands.

It had been the greatest night of her life – and the most shattering. Any small earlier triumphs paled into insignificance beside what had happened this evening. She had scored a sensational success before a knowledgeable and largely influential audience. The fact that Oscar Warrender considered her worthy of his personal recommendation to Dermot Deane was some measure of the impact she had made. And Jonathan Keyne wanted her for his Canadian tour – if it ever took place.

That was something, wasn't it? Six months ago she would have been mad with joy to be selected by Jonathan Keyne for such a tour. He didn't *have* to be in love with her. Only a romantic fool expected to mix sentiment with a career. What was she agonising about? She had been made the kind of offer every artist dreamed of. And here she was crying – she was surprised to find that she was crying – because the little bit of romantic gilt which he had added to the gingerbread probably had an ulterior motive behind it.

"Pull yourself together!" she admonished herself. "And try to grow a decently tough skin. This may not be the beginning of a great romance. But it could be the beginning of a great career."

In the next few days she almost convinced herself that this was all that mattered to her. The reviews of the concert, when they came – on the Thursday morning, as Teresa had prophesied – were uniformly good, and in some cases so lavish in their praise of both the work and the soloist that, as her father said, "We couldn't have done more if we'd written them ourselves!"

Again people telephoned from all over the place to congratulate her, and her friend Judy Edmonds even telephoned from London.

"Oh, Anna, bless you! You made it – you made it! You transported them. Remember what I said about that quality which you have?"

"I remembered all the time I was singing, Judy."

"Did you really?" Judy was evidently immeasurably gratified.

"Yes. I just felt something rising within me, and I knew that was IT, and that I was crossing the line between a good performer and an artist. It's a most extraordinary feeling, but thrilling!"

"I can't wait to discuss it all," Judy declared. "When am I going to see you?"

"I'll be in London on Monday. Oscar Warrender is arranging for Dermot Deane to hear me on Tuesday or Wednesday."

"Just say that again, will you?" Judy begged.

Anna did so, and there was a little squeak of excitement from the other end.

"Do you remember when *you* envied *me* just because I saw Oscar Warrender in the office and heard him talk about Jonathan Keyne? You've come a long way since then, Anna, and pretty fast."

"Yes, I've been incredibly lucky," Anna agreed earnestly.

"Not just luck! Years of hard devoted work behind it too," Judy declared. "What is the latest news on Jonathan Keyne, incidentally? Didn't he have something to do with your local festival?"

"Well – " Anna hesitated, unwilling to embark on that subject on the phone. Then she said virtuously, "Shouldn't we stop now? You must be spending a fortune telephoning from London during the day."

"It's all right. I'm on the office phone – with full permission."

"Isn't that surprisingly generous of them?" said Anna in astonishment.

"No. We're music publishers, remember. I just told them I was the best friend of Kenneth Fulroyd's daughter, and suggested it might be a good thing for me to move in on the connection right away. It worked like magic."

"Judy, did it?" Anna was almost awed as she saw what amazing vistas might be opening out for her father as well as herself. "How – how unbelievable life has become!"

"Well, tell me about Jonathan Keyne's part in your unbelievable life," Judy urged.

"Not now. I'll tell you everything when I see you," declared Anna. And if she had certain mental reservations about exactly what "everything" might mean, she found she was longing for a marathon talk with Judy once more. "Come to the flat on Monday evening and we'll go out somewhere to eat."

On that she rang off, and went to find her father, who was still poring over the reviews.

"I must take these all over to your mother this afternoon," he said without looking up.

"Then I'll come too, of course! I must see Mother before I go to London, anyway."

So there was a happy and triumphant family discussion that afternoon, and for a few hours Anna almost believed that there was no cloud on her happiness after all.

She felt differently, however, when she returned home and the invaluable Mrs. Ford stated that two gentlemen had been there enquiring for her.

"Together?" asked Anna.

"Oh, no!" Mrs. Ford's tone said clearly that each had obviously wished to see Anna very much on her own. "The first was young Mr. Delawney. He was disappointed not to find you, but said he would phone later and wanted you to drive to London with him on Sunday."

"I can't," said Anna, immediately and rather defensively.

Mrs. Ford made no comment on that but, consulting a pad on which she had evidently made notes, went on, "The other gentleman said his name was Mr. Keyne. He was disappointed too, I think. He said to tell you he had to go to London this evening and he wanted to know where he could find you there. But I couldn't tell him. That was when he seemed very disappointed."

"It doesn't matter, Mrs. Ford," declared Anna airily and quite untruthfully.

"Doesn't it?" said Mrs. Ford. "He was a nice young man."

It was Anna who withheld comment that time. And when Rod telephoned later that evening with his offer of the lift to London she replied, with almost unnecessary firmness, that long car journeys tired her, and she would be going on Monday morning by train. She then told herself she was glad not to have to bother with either of them. And she almost believed that too.

When it actually came to leaving home she found there was a lump in her throat. During those long, anxious — and then wonderful — weeks she had grown very close to her father, and her home town would always now be the place to be remembered nostalgically as the scene of her first great triumph.

But once the good-byes had been said and the train was rushing her on her way, she found her thoughts were running eagerly ahead. To London, which she had always loved, and where Warrender and Dermot Deane, fresh work and perhaps further triumphs, were awaiting her. Jonathan too, of course. But she tried to pretend to herself that he represented no more than a possible further step forward in her career. Any personal feelings about him must not be allowed to enter into the picture.

When she arrived at the flat there were friendly greetings from the other girls. But her world was so far removed from theirs that their interest in her success was largely academic. They were slightly impressed, it was true, by the fact that there was a letter waiting for her from the famous Oscar Warrender. But their reaction would have been much the same had he been a footballer of note or a disc jockey.

The letter — of no more than half a dozen lines — told her to be at the Carrington Studios once more the following afternoon at three o'clock, and Anna would have been less than human if she had not exulted in the thought of how much her life had changed since she last sang there.

Not until Judy joined her that evening was she able to

describe at length for a passionately interested listener the experiences which had been hers in the months she had been away. They sat for hours in a small Italian restaurant, where the proprietor was indulgent towards young things who needed to tell each other their life stories.

Anna enjoyed answering most of Judy's questions, and when inevitably the question about Jonathan Keyne was repeated, she was able to say in all innocence that he had indeed had a good deal to do with the Festival, since he was a special friend of Teresa Delawney.

"I didn't see an awful lot of him until the famous concert when Dad and I made the headlines," she explained truthfully, "but he was very complimentary then. In fact, he brought up the question of his Canadian tour again and, if it comes off, I think he wants me to be in the company."

"What do you mean – 'if it comes off'?"

"There's some difficulty about financing it, I understand, and it may be necessary to postpone it for a while. Mr. Warrender says it would mean good experience for me if it does materialise, but that I mustn't count on anything until it actually happens. Which is just common sense, of course. If Dermot Deane takes me on, it will mean that he will look for engagements for me, so it wouldn't do to tie myself up too much in advance."

"But surely you'd put the Canadian tour with Keyne before almost anything else, wouldn't you?" exclaimed Judy.

And the moment that was said Anna knew how willingly – *how* willingly – she would do just that. The very idea of turning down that tour in favour of anything else was absurd. With the situation put in a nutshell like that, she saw her assumed indifference for what it was. Just a piece of silly bluff which did not deceive even herself.

"Yes," she said slowly, "I suppose I would put Jonathan's Canadian tour before almost anything else."

"Do you call him Jonathan to his face?" asked Judy curiously. And when Anna nodded, she went on, "And do you call Warrender Oscar?"

"Oh, no!" Anna sounded genuinely shocked. "No one but his wife does that, I imagine."

"I'm glad," said Judy unexpectedly. "I don't like it when the Olympians get all chummy with every Tom, Dick and Harry. It destroys their star quality, in my opinion. Though I shall still expect to call you Anna even when you're a prima donna at Covent Garden!"

They both laughed over that, and fell into a happy mood of casting Anna in imagination for various Covent Garden roles, until Judy looked at her watch and said Anna had better have an early night, after her long journey.

"You'll need to be fresh for tomorrow's audition," she declared. "And I expect you'll be going to Madame Marburger in the morning for a bit of extra coaching."

Anna said that she certainly was. And at last, reluctantly, they parted.

In spite of genuine weariness, it took Anna a long time to fall asleep. Not only did brilliant scenes from a possible future dance before her eyes, but her mind went back to unforgettable moments in the past; in every one of which Jonathan had been involved. Particularly she thought again and again of that first time she had gone to the Carrington Studios to sing for him. Well, at least this time he would not be there.

She was quite wrong, however. No sooner had she entered the studio that next afternoon than she realised there were three men waiting to hear her. Warrender, a stout, knowledgeable-looking man she recognised as the famous Dermot Deane – and Jonathan Keyne.

Anna hesitated a moment and then walked forward, her heart thumping unnecessarily hard. Warrender introduced Dermot Deane. Then, as he seemed to think Jonathan's presence required no explanation, Anna said as casually as she could,

"Hello, Jonathan. I didn't know you were coming along."

"Nor did I." He smiled full at her in that compelling way. "But I ran into Deane this morning and he happened to mention this audition, and I explained I had a watching brief on your career and would like to come too."

"A watching brief?" Anna permitted herself a look of some surprise. But Warrender cut across this unnecessary verbal exchange with the remark that they were all busy people and perhaps Anna would tell him what she wished to sing, as he was himself going to accompany her.

Oddly enough, this did not have the effect of putting Anna off her stroke. On the contrary, it stiffened her professional backbone. So she produced her music, had a word or two of discussion with the conductor and then went, completely relaxed, to stand in the curve of the grand piano.

"Turn to face me," he ordered. "You aren't yet capable of managing entirely on your own."

She turned obediently so that she could see his handsome, expressive face, and was glad to find that this meant she need not look in Jonathan's direction.

She sang a lesser-known aria of Handel's, then one of Susanna's airs, and finally Musetta's Waltz Song, with which she had created such a good impression in this studio before.

Dermot Deane said nothing at all until she had finished, then he merely observed to Warrender, "Yes, I see what you mean." And to Anna – "Do you sing any songs?"

"What sort of songs?" asked Anna doubtfully.

"Anything. German lied, French chanson – even an English ballad."

"I sing Berlioz's 'L'Absence'," said Anna obligingly.

"Oh, come! That's quite a good test," replied Dermot Deane, obviously a good deal amused at this modest way of offering one of the most difficult songs in the repertoire.

"I haven't got the music with me."

"I can sketch in the accompaniment, I think," Warrender said. "What key?"

She told him and he began to play. Anna knew it was rash of her to attempt this song before such a knowledgeable trio. But when she took the magical rising phrase without a quiver, she sensed that they were all approving.

At the end Dermot Deane observed, "One could make a recitalist of her eventually."

"Eventually, but not for a long time," retorted Warrender. "That's the last stage."

"There are so few good recitalists today for a wretched manager to handle," sighed Dermot Deane.

"Of course," said Warrender coldly. "Every little warbler thinks she can choose her own party pieces, inflict them on the public and call herself a recitalist. They scratch the surface of one great song after another without the faintest idea of the real meaning. Don't you dare push this girl into concert work yet."

"Not against your advice," Dermot Deane smiled. "Oratorio, I think, and some minor operatic roles if I can get her in."

"She's due for operatic roles with me in Canada early

169

next summer," stated Jonathan at that point.

"It's not absolutely settled," Anna heard herself say. And she suddenly felt sick as she saw the patent dismay in his eyes. She had not meant him to give himself away as badly as that.

"I thought it was a promise," he said, and his tone was just the least bit harsh.

"Rather a lightly spoken one." She looked coolly at him. "And that was before I knew I was to sing for Mr. Deane."

"But, Anna –"

"I suggest we hold our discussions of actual engagements until I've got Miss Fulroyd under contract and we can talk on a proper business footing," cut in Dermot Deane smoothly. "Can you come to my office tomorrow, Miss Fulroyd? – No, not tomorrow, I have to go to Paris. Say Thursday morning at eleven-thirty?"

"Yes, indeed." Anna spoke eagerly, and she studiedly avoided Jonathan's glance.

Then Deane clapped Jonathan genially on the shoulder and said, "All right, I'm not going to sell her to any rival of yours. This is just business. Can I give you a lift? My car is outside."

"No, thank you," replied Jonathan. But Warrender said he was going Deane's way, and before Anna realised what was happening, the two men had bade her good-bye and were going out, leaving her alone with Jonathan.

She gathered up her music with almost feverish haste, and made to follow them with all speed. But Jonathan's hand on her arm – none too gently – stopped her, and his voice said rather grimly, "Just a moment. What are you playing at this time, Anna?"

"I'm not playing at anything! What do you mean?" She shook off his hand impatiently.

"You know very well what I mean. That promise was not at all lightly given. Nothing we said to each other in the car that night was lightly meant – or so I thought. Why have you suddenly turned round and played hard to get, both artistically and personally?"

"I haven't – " she began. And then, with a cold shock of awareness, she realised all at once that this was the moment of truth. "It's quite simple, Jonathan," she said deliberately. "I just happened to find out why you really wanted me in your company."

She wished he wouldn't look so deathly startled. It made her feel almost sick again. But he recovered himself and said angrily, "I want you because you're one of the best singers I've heard in years. Isn't that sufficient reason?"

"If that were the only reason – yes. But there is another, isn't there? I'm not quite so – dumb as you seem to think."

He stared at her for a moment as though he could not believe he had heard aright. Then he flushed a dark red, like a schoolboy found out in a lie.

She waited, feeling horrible. And then, to her unspeakable dismay, he laughed and shrugged, as though they were dealing with something which could be dismissed as easily as that.

"So what?" He actually smiled defiantly at her. "Is there anything so criminal about it?"

"Not criminal," she said quietly. "Just utterly unacceptable." And she made a brief little gesture as though wiping her hands of something unwelcome. Then she picked up her music again and, with her legs trembling more than she would have believed possible, she went out of the room.

If he had followed her she didn't know what she

would have done. But he did not follow her. And mercifully there was a taxi immediately outside the Studios. She got in, gasped out her address and almost collapsed on the worn leather seat.

She should not have been so brutal. She could have left some of that unsaid and still have achieved her purpose. But, she told herself, it was when he gave that defiant smile that she had seen him at last for what he was. He was not even *ashamed* of what he had done.

All right – he needed that money desperately, and Rod Delawney was willing to supply it, on the distinct understanding that she should be a member of the company. Up to that point, the situation was just bearable. But that he should have made instant love to her in order to make sure of his subsidy – that was inexcusable! And, judging from that smiling little shrug, he didn't even *know* it was inexcusable.

When she reached home she went straight to her room, although all the other girls were out. She felt she could not shut herself away sufficiently from the rest of the world while she lived through this miserable hour of revelation. And there she sat, beside her bed, telling herself that, horribly though this hurt, it was best that she should know the truth now and so armour herself against anything else that Jonathan could do to her.

"He's not the only man in the world," she told herself. "He's not even the only man in my life." And she thought, with a sort of anguished relief, of gay, kind Rod Delawney, whose madly generous offer had precipitated this crisis and, strangely enough, shown up Jonathan for what he was.

"I've always taken Rod too casually for granted," she thought remorsefully. "And all the time he was worth three of Jonathan Keyne. If only –"

And at that moment the telephone bell rang. She was half inclined to let it go on ringing, in case it should be Jonathan telephoning with fresh excuses. Then the odd idea came to her that perhaps her very thinking so intensely of him had prompted Rod to telephone. And when she went into the hall and lifted the receiver, she was not entirely surprised to hear his voice asking for her.

"Oh, Rod! It's Anna speaking."

"Darling girl, what luck to find you in! What are you doing this evening?"

"N-nothing," she said, more forlornly than she knew.

"You are, you know. You're coming out with me. Meet me in the lounge at the Gloria in half an hour, and we'll have a drink and decide where we're going and what we're going to do."

"That would be wonderful!" she exclaimed, and she meant it, For to sit at home and think about Jonathan would be agony. To go out with Rod, accepting him fully at last for the delightful fellow he was, would be comfort unspeakable.

She promised to be with him in half an hour, and then rushed away to don her prettiest dress and a little fur jacket, which she drew close up to her throat to protect the precious voice of which she was now more than ever aware.

In spite of the rush, she was, she knew, looking her best as she walked into the lounge of the Gloria only five minutes after the specified time. And Rod was there to welcome her, install her in a secluded corner seat, and then listen with the utmost interest to her account of the audition for Dermot Deane.

"Was there anyone else there besides Warrender and Deane?" he wanted to know.

"Jonathan was there," she said, and then found she

could say no more.

"Oh – " he laughed slightly, "Jonathan Keyne."

"Why do you laugh like that, Rod?"

"I don't know. Perhaps because the thought of him makes me feel slightly uncomfortable."

"I don't think it need," she said earnestly. "You mean because of your generous offer to help finance his tour on – on terms?"

He nodded, and swirled the whisky round in his glass, regarding it with a dry little smile.

"Rod," she exclaimed on sudden impulse, "what did he *say* exactly, when you made the offer?"

"Does it matter?"

"Yes, it – it does rather."

"Well, he didn't say anything at all at first, Anna. It was made on impulse, you know, almost between snatches of conversation as we were all leaving the church after the concert."

"And then he – he referred to it again?"

"Yes, he did. Much later that evening, when I returned from taking you and your father home."

She caught her breath. By then, of course, Jonathan had sounded her out and knew her reaction.

"What did he say then?" she pressed, hating to hear the whole story, yet knowing she must submit herself to it.

"He asked me if I had made the offer in all seriousness, and I assured him I had."

"And then – ?"

"Then, Anna," said Rod, still swirling the whisky in his glass, "he refused the offer. And I'm bound to say in terms that made me rather ashamed that I'd ever made it."

CHAPTER NINE

"He – refused? Jonathan *refused* your offer of financial backing?" Anna stared at Rod Delawney in stupefaction and she thought for a moment she was going to faint. "You can't mean it. You must be mistaken."

"Oh, no, I'm not! He couldn't have been more offensively explicit." Rod made a half-humorous grimace. "In fact, if I were not a peaceable sort of chap, I'd probably have felt impelled to punch his head. Anyway, what are you worrying about? The possibility of your tour falling through? You needn't, you know. He's expecting to get the backing from some other quarter, isn't he?"

"I – I don't know," stammered Anna, making a tremendous effort to recover her composure and look as though her dismay went no further than her anxiety about the tour. "Is he? Who is supplying it – do you know?"

"He didn't offer any information. He wasn't exactly in an expansive mood." Rod grinned, his natural good humour obviously now conquering his remembered resentment. "My guess is that Warrender has something to do with it –"

"Oscar Warrender? But *does* he back anything of that kind?"

"I shouldn't think so – in the ordinary way. But he has considerable faith in Keyne's future, if he's given a chance. Like all of us, if I'm frank, I think he felt it was a damned shame that old Nat Bretherton behaved the way he did. And, provided he wasn't left to carry the whole can, I think Warrender would bestir himself on behalf of someone as gifted as Keyne."

"Do you think he could possibly afford it?" Anna asked doubtfully.

"Warrender? How much do you suppose *he's* worth?" Rod retorted amusedly. "Well, no – of course he wouldn't do the whole thing on his own, as I said. But I should think he might be willing to be a heavy shareholder if someone else proposed the idea."

"Who else?"

Rod rubbed his chin reflectively and said, "I wouldn't put it past my own mamma to have a hand in it."

"Your mother? You mean your father, don't you?"

"No, no. My father wouldn't be prepared to put up any more after the Festival."

"Not even for Teresa?" She could not help saying that.

"Teresa would expect to make her own terms, you know," replied Rod drily. "And I think Jonathan had indicated in the politest way possible that they would not be acceptable."

"Do you?" Somehow there was the smallest crumb of comfort somewhere in that statement. "But what makes you think your mother could – or would – help?"

"Several things. None of which may be right, of course. I'm only guessing, really. But I know her very well. We tick in rather the same way in lots of things. She's a very independent-minded woman, my mother. Even so far as her family is concerned if she feels strongly. In addition –" he gave that genuinely amused grin again – "I don't know quite how to put this, but there's a degree of competitiveness between her and Teresa, you know. Well, Teresa has had her fun with the Festival. I could well imagine Mother countering with an opera tour – particularly if it took Jonathan out of Teresa's orbit. She never approved of Teresa's efforts in that direction."

"Do you mean that she disapproved on Teresa's behalf
– or Jonathan's?"

"Both, I shouldn't wonder," replied Rod promptly.
"With the snobbish side of her she wants Teresa to marry
a title eventually. With what you might call the human
side of her she has quite enough acumen to know that
Teresa would be death to Jonathan as an artist."

"You can say that of your own sister?" Anna was
shocked, and could not help showing it.

He smiled good-humouredly, but she noticed for the
first time what a determined line there was to his jaw.

"My dear Anna, as a complete realist, most certainly I
can say that of Teresa, because it's true. You don't suppose the Delawneys make their money by being senti-
mentally blind about people, do you? Not even their
nearest and dearest. I'm quite fond of Teresa in my way,
and I greatly admire her talents, but I have no illusions
about her."

"Oh," said Anna, and then for a minute she was silent,
digesting what was to her an extraordinary family
attitude. Finally she drew an involuntary sigh and said,
"So you think your mother may have offered Jonathan
financial backing? It's a great deal of money for a woman
to put up, isn't it, even if other people are involved?"

"She could afford a pretty handsome gesture, if she
felt so inclined," Rod assured her carelessly. "And, like
the rest of us, she knows how to influence useful people.
If she really had Warrender's support – and I notice
they had a good deal to say to each other at one time or
another – she would know how to make the idea attractive in the right quarters."

"So that's how it's done!" Anna smiled faintly.

"Yes, Anna, that's how it's done." He laughed. "There
would be a good deal of discussion first, of course – which

would explain why Jonathan is not absolutely sure he has it all in the bag yet. But my guess is that he'll bring it off all right. So there was no need for you to look so dismayed, my dear. That tour will take place – and you will be the star of it."

She forced what she hoped he would take to be a happy, relieved laugh, and then called on all her acting powers to appear carefree instead of beset – as she was – by tearing remorse and anxiety.

Fortunately for her, a few moments later a waiter came to say that Mr. Delawney was wanted on the telephone, and with a word of excuse to her he went away, leaving her in her secluded corner, free for a moment to re-examine with feverish dismay the situation she had created between Jonathan and herself.

He was innocent. Jonathan was completely innocent of the contemptible behaviour she had attributed to him. Far from making love to her for a paltry ulterior motive, he had refused the money on which all his plans depended, rather than compromise her interests in the slightest degree.

Considered in that light, the scene she had made that afternoon appeared so crassly idiotic that she writhed even to think of it. What must he have thought when she accused him of wanting her in this company for any reason other than the very obvious one that she was a good singer? No wonder he had looked astounded!

But then he had flushed deeply. And that was what had seemed to her to seal his guilt. He had looked so exactly as though she had found him out in something. It couldn't have been sheer anger – justified though that would have been. It surely meant only one thing – that he did want her with him because he loved her. It was real – it was real!

For a few seconds she experienced such an uprush of happiness and relief that everything else was forgotten. But then, with icy dismay, she remembered how she had received this misunderstood declaration. She had almost literally wiped her hands of him and informed him brutally that the whole thing was "utterly unacceptable".

"I must explain to him! I must find him somehow and explain to him," she thought wildly. And she had actually risen to her feet, when the sight of Rod returning across the room reminded her that she was not yet a free agent. She must put on her mask of calm sociability once more. She had had her few moments of respite – if that was what it could be called – and now she must listen to his plans for the evening, having so eagerly accepted his invitation less than an hour ago.

What he had planned was a charming dinner – to which she managed somehow to do reasonable justice – and then a night at the opera, where there was a new production of "Carmen", with Nicholas Brenner in the part of Don José.

"Oh, Rod, how clever of you to get seats!" For a moment her joy was genuine. "I've only heard him once before, and that was just from the slips, where you don't see much, though you hear marvellously."

"Well, you'll see everything tonight," Rod promised her. "We're in the fifth row of the stalls."

"Is Warrender conducting?"

It seemed Warrender was not conducting that night. But a few minutes after they had taken their seats, Anna saw him and Anthea come into a first tier box. She just had time to whisper this piece of information to Rod before the conductor for the evening entered the orchestra pit and the performance began.

For the first few minutes Anna still thought about her

own tangled affairs. But then the compulsion of the drama laid its hand upon her, and presently she was utterly absorbed in the duet between José and Micaela, only digressing for a moment to think just how *she* would like to do Micaela when the time came.

In the pregnant pause before Carmen made her entrance, for some reason or other Anna glanced up again at the Warrenders' box, and then she saw that Jonathan had joined them. The entrance of the justly famous Carmen was completely lost on her. Ashamed she might be of that later in the evening, but in that first moment she could think only that Jonathan was in the house.

During the first interval she let Rod take her out and give her coffee, but she caught no glimpse of Jonathan or the Warrenders. Possibly, of course, they had gone round backstage. In the second interval too there was no sign of them, and when Rod suggested that they should go upstairs to the crush bar, she refused in near-panic. For if they saw the Warrenders and Jonathan inevitably they would have to join them, and what was there that he and she could say to each other while other people stood by?

Just as they were about to return to their seats, one of the Opera House staff, who evidently knew Rod, came up to him with a slip of paper.

"This phone message just came through for you, Mr. Delawney."

"Thanks – " Rod took the message, read it and frowned. "Anna, I'm frightfully sorry – " he turned to her – "I'll just have to miss this act. There's a bit of a South American crisis on, and we're involved financially. I must go to the office – "

"At this hour?"

"I'm afraid so. Financial crises don't go by the clock.

I'll get back if I possibly can before the end of the performance. But if not, I'll arrange with the Sergeant to put you into a taxi. I hate to leave you like this, but – "

"It's all right, Rod." She smiled at him understandingly, and managed to conceal the relief she felt at being left on her own at last, with no necessity to play a part any more.

"Good girl!" He kissed her lightly and left her. And Anna went back into the house, to be harrowed by Nicholas Brenner's portrayal of the ruined José, and the anxious conviction that she also had probably ruined her life.

At the end she slowly made her way out into the foyer, holding back for a scared moment of concealment when she saw Jonathan hurry down the big main staircase and out into the night. She should have had the courage to stop him – but she had not. And now he had gone.

She stood there utterly undecided, and suddenly Anthea Warrender's voice said behind her, "Hello! I thought I saw you in the house, but somehow we didn't meet up during the intervals."

"No. I – I – " She turned to greet them.

"Jonathan has just gone to get the car," Anthea explained. "Are you alone? We could give you a lift. I'm sure Jonathan would be glad to."

"No, he wouldn't," said Anna before she could stop herself. "I mean – "

"Is he in your bad books at the moment?" enquired Warrender with a touch of genuine interest.

"It isn't that. I'm in his. And – and it serves me right – " Then Anna stopped, appalled to find she had been unable to hold back exactly what was in her mind.

Both the Warrenders looked slightly taken aback for a moment. Then Anthea said kindly, "One can always say one is sorry. I do sometimes. And even Oscar does very, very occasionally."

"But not in front of other people," observed Warrender, with that almost uncanny perception which was one of his special gifts. "Is that the trouble, Anna?"

She nodded wordlessly. But then, as they reached the doorway and she saw Jonathan's car moving up in the queue, she said quickly, "I must go. Thank you, but – "

"Just a moment." To her boundless surprise, the great conductor's hand closed round her arm, and only then did she realise how strong his fingers were. As always, the crowds parted instinctively before him, and she found herself quite effortlessly propelled out on to the pavement, just as Jonathan's car drew up.

"Mr. Warrender, please – " she whispered urgently.

But he merely bent down to open the car door and speak to the astonished Jonathan.

"Anthea and I have to go backstage, after all," he stated smoothly. "But here's Anna Fulroyd needing a lift. Perhaps you would take her – and join us at the Gloria later."

And before Anna – or, to tell the truth, Jonathan either – could do anything about it, she had been handed into the car, the door was shut and the next car coming up behind was hooting for them to move on.

They moved on – in deathly silence – and not until they were clear of the crowds did Jonathan say, in a tone she had never heard from him before, "What is this, exactly? A hijacking?"

"No – no," she assured him feverishly. "It wasn't my idea. It was Mr. Warrender's."

"And a pretty poor idea too, if I may say so."

"He – he meant it kindly," she stammered in all fairness.

"To whom? It was no kindness to me, I assure you."

"I know – I know." Her voice shook so that she had great difficulty in getting out a complete sentence. "Jonathan, please, please can we go somewhere quiet where you can stop the car and we can talk?"

"Why? I have absolutely nothing to say to you," he stated with brutal precision.

"But I have to you," she cried desperately.

"I can't imagine what." But he headed the car north, in the general direction of Regents Park.

She was not quite sure if it were relief at having gained one small point or fear of what lay ahead, but she found tears on her cheeks and had the greatest difficulty in wiping them away surreptitiously. She evidently made a bad job of her small, furtive movement because, still looking ahead, he said,

"Stop crying. Tears are always a bore. And you make me nervous."

"*You*?" she exclaimed indignantly. "How do you suppose *I'm* feeling?"

"I have no idea. And I'm not even trying to guess. This idiotic interview was your choice, not mine."

"Jonathan, it's quiet here. Won't you stop the car?"

He stopped the car and sat staring straight ahead.

"I want to tell you – I want to tell you it was all a mistake this afternoon –"

"Was it?" There was nothing encouraging about his tone.

"Yes. You see – Jonathan, please *look* at me. I can't just talk to a profile. It was a mistake –"

"You've said that before." Still he wouldn't look at her. "And frankly, there've been too many mistakes where you and I are concerned. I'm finally and absolutely sick of them. You're not the girl I thought you were. You're just –"

"But I am! I am! Look at me, Jonathan – " suddenly she put her arms round him. "I *am* the same. I'm Anna – Don't treat me like a stranger. Don't you remember – ?"

And then suddenly he turned his head and looked at her, and the incredible thing he said was, " 'Manon'. That's what you ought to play! That's exactly the way she should hang round the wretched Des Grieux. You have the voice and the looks and the – the beguiling ways. You'd be the perfect Manon! Did no one ever tell you?"

"I don't *want* to be the perfect Manon! She was a hussy, anyway," cried Anna, really in tears by now. "I'm talking about me – about us. I don't want to talk about a stupid opera."

" 'Manon' isn't a stupid opera. It's one of the loveliest in the repertoire. And she was a honey in her maddening way, and could make a fool of any man. Is that what you want to do with me? – make a fool of me again?" And he kissed her hard on her lips.

"No!" She clung to him with an abandon that any Manon might have envied. "I just want to tell you that I love you, and that was why I was wild this afternoon. I thought you'd just pretended to make love to me because you wanted Rod Delawney's money, and I didn't know – "

"Hush, hush, hush! Don't cry like that." Suddenly he had her in his arms and was actually rocking her gently to and fro. "Just say that all over again quite slowly – particularly the bit about loving me. Though if you really do love me, why the hell do you treat me like this? I felt suicidal all the evening, and understood exactly why José finally killed the girl he loved. Now tell me again about you and me and Rod Delawney, and let's get it straight, once and for all."

So, close in his arms, and interrupting herself with the occasional sob even now, she told him how she had misjudged him and how that had led her to behave so abominably to him.

"And you really thought I was that sort of a heel?" he said at last.

"No, I didn't think you were. But it seemed that you *must* be."

"Amounts to the same thing," he told her. "You really have been a bit of a goose, haven't you?"

"Yes," she said humbly, at which he kissed her and added thoughtfully,

"Well, I suppose I was a fool too. I ought to have beaten you and insisted on making you see the truth."

"Yes," she agreed happily again. And this time she kissed him.

"What does it all add up to?" he said, stroking her cheek. "Just tell me in simple words that allow of no second meaning, can you?"

She nodded and wiped away the last tears.

"I love you," she said with a gulp. "And I want desperately to be in your Canadian company, and I don't care about anything Dermot Deane gets for me so long as I can be with you. And even if there's no Canadian tour, I still want to be with you. And – and that's all."

"It's enough, my dear, dear, no-longer-muddled little Anna," he told her tenderly, and kissed the tip of her nose. "And now we're going to drive back to the Gloria together and tell the Warrenders all about it."

"But they aren't expecting me," she said quickly.

"If I know Warrender, he's expecting you all right," replied Jonathan with a laugh. "He's probably got his stop-watch out now, and fancying himself as the *deus ex machina*. Why do you suppose he shoved you into this car with me?"

"Oh, yes – I see." She smiled slowly, and he kissed her

again and turned the car and began to drive back to town.

At the Gloria he allowed her a few minutes to do some running repairs to her face and remove the last trace of tears. Then hand-in-hand they went into the big dining-room and stood looking round.

"Here they come," observed Warrender to his wife, in a tone of some satisfaction. "It's all right, he has brought her too. We shan't have the Canadian tour scuppered, after all."

"Is *that* all you care about?" exclaimed Anthea reproachfully.

"What else?" Her famous husband looked amused. But she studied him thoughtfully with her head slightly on one side.

"You know what I think, Oscar," she said at last. "I think underneath all that Warrender build-up you're just a romantic at heart."

"And if I am, whose fault do you think that is?" replied Warrender, and he smiled at his wife across the table before he rose to welcome the two who were approaching them.

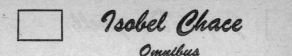

Isobel Chace
Omnibus

A writer of romance is a weaver of dreams. This is true of ISOBEL CHACE, and her many thousands of ardent readers can attest to this. All of her eagerly anticipated works are so carefully spun, blending the mystery and the beauty of love.

. . . . CONTAINING

A HANDFUL OF SILVER . . . set in the exciting city of Rio de Janeiro, with its endless beaches and tall skyscraper hotels, and where a battle of wits is being waged between Madeleine Delahaye, Pilar Fernandez the lovely but jealous fiancee of her childhood friend, and her handsome, treacherous cousin — the strange Luis da Maestro . . . (#1306).

THE SAFFRON SKY . . . takes us to a tiny village skirting the exotic Bangkok, Siam, bathed constantly in glorious sunshine, where at night the sky changes to an enchanting saffron colour. The small nervous Myfanwy Jones realizes her most cherished dream, adventure and romance in a far off land. In Siam, two handsome men are determined to marry her — but, they both have the same mysterious reason . . . (#1250).

THE DAMASK ROSE . . . in Damascus, the original Garden of Eden, we are drenched in the heady atmosphere of exotic perfumes, when Vickie Tremaine flies from London to work for Perfumes of Damascus and meets Adam Templeton, fiancee of the young rebellious Miriam, and alas as the weeks pass, Vickie only becomes more attracted to this your Englishman with the steel-like personality . . . (#1334).

$1.50 per volume

Violet Winspear
Omnibus

"To be able to reproduce the warmly exciting world of romance . . . a colourful means of escape", this was the ambition of the young VIOLET WINSPEAR, now a world famous author. Here, we offer three moving stories in which she has well and truly achieved this.

. . . . CONTAINING

PALACE OF THE PEACOCKS . . . where we join young Temple Lane, in the ridiculous predicament of masquerading as a youth on an old tub of a steamer, somewhere in the Java Seas. She had saved for five years to join her fiancee in this exotic world of blue skies and peacock waters — and now . . . she must escape him . . . (#1318).

BELOVED TYRANT . . . takes us to Monterey, where high mountainous country is alive with scents and bird-song above the dark blue surge of the Pacific Ocean. Here, we meet Lyn Gilmore, Governess at the Hacienda Rosa, where she falls victim to the tyranny of the ruthless, savagely handsome, Rick Corderas . . . (#1032).

COURT OF THE VEILS . . . is set in a lush plantation on the edge of the Sahara Desert, where Roslyn Brant faces great emotional conflict, for not only has she lost all recollection of her fiancee and her past, but the ruthless Duane Hunter refuses to believe that she ever was engaged to marry his handsome cousin . . . (#1267).

$1.50 per volume

Joyce Dingwell

Omnibus

JOYCE DINGWELL'S lighthearted style of writing and her delightful characters are well loved by a great many readers all over the world. An author with the unusual combination of compassion and vitality which she generously shares with the reader, in all of her books.

. . . . CONTAINING

THE FEEL OF SILK . . . Faith Blake, a young Australian nurse becomes stranded in the Orient and is very kindly offered the position of nursing the young niece of the Marques Jacinto de Velira. But, as Faith and a young doctor become closer together, the Marques begins to take an unusual interest in Faith's private life . . . (#1342).

A TASTE FOR LOVE . . . here we join Gina Lake, at Bancroft Bequest, a remote children's home at Orange Hills, Australia, just as she is nearing the end of what has been a very long "engagement" to Tony Mallory, who seems in no hurry to marry. The new superintendent, Miles Fairland however, feels quite differently as Gina is about to discover . . . (#1229).

WILL YOU SURRENDER . . . at Galdang Academy for boys, "The College By The Sea", perched on the cliff edge of an Australian headland, young Gerry Prosset faces grave disappointment when her father is passed over and young Damien Manning becomes the new Headmaster. Here we learn of her bitter resentment toward this young man — and moreso, the woman who comes to visit him . . . (#1179).

$1.50 per volume

Susan Barrie

Omnibus

The charming, unmistakable works of SUSAN BARRIE, one of the top romance authors, have won her a reward of endless readers who take the greatest of pleasure from her inspiring stories, always told with the most enchanting locations.

. . . . CONTAINING

MARRY A STRANGER . . . Doctor Martin Guelder sought only a housekeeper and hostess for his home, Fountains Court, in the village of Herfordshire in the beautiful English countryside. Young Stacey Brent accepts his proposal, but soon finds herself falling deeply in love with him — and she cannot let him know . . . (#1043).

THE MARRIAGE WHEEL . . . at Farthing Hall, a delightful old home nestled in the quiet countryside of Gloucestershire, we meet Frederica Wells, chauffeur to Lady Allerdale. In need of more financial security, Frederica takes a second post, to work for Mr. Humphrey Lestrode, an exacting and shrewd businessman. Almost immediately — she regrets it . . . (#1311).

ROSE IN THE BUD . . . Venice, city of romantic palaces, glimmering lanterns and a thousand waterways. In the midst of all this beauty, Catherine Brown is in search of the truth about the mysterious disappearance of her step-sister. Her only clue is a portrait of the girl, which she finds in the studio of the irresistably attractive Edouard Moroc — could it be that he knows of her whereabouts? . . . (#1168).

$1.50 per volume